RESISTING
MISS MERRYWEATHER

OTHER WORKS

THE BALEFUL GODMOTHER SERIES

THE FEY QUARTET (SERIES PREQUEL)

MAYTHORN'S WISH
HAZEL'S PROMISE
IVY'S CHOICE
LARKSPUR'S QUEST

ORIGINAL SERIES

UNMASKING MISS APPLEBY
RESISTING MISS MERRYWEATHER
TRUSTING MISS TRENTHAM
CLAIMING MISTER KEMP
RUINING MISS WROTHAM
DISCOVERING MISS DALRYMPLE

OTHER HISTORICAL ROMANCES

THE COUNTESS'S GROOM
THE SPINSTER'S SECRET

FANTASY NOVELS (WRITTEN AS EMILY GEE)

THIEF WITH NO SHADOW
THE LAURENTINE SPY

THE CURSED KINGDOMS TRILOGY
THE SENTINEL MAGE ~ *THE FIRE PRINCE* ~ *THE BLOOD CURSE*

RESISTING
MISS MERRYWEATHER

Emily Larkin

A Baleful Godmother

Novella

www.emilylarkin.com

Publisher's Note: This is a work of fiction. Names, characters, places, and incidents are a product of the author's imagination. Locales and public names are sometimes used for atmospheric purposes. Any resemblance to actual people, living or dead, or to businesses, companies, events, institutions, or locales is completely coincidental.

Book Layout © 2014 BookDesignTemplates.com

Cover Design: The Killion Group, Inc

Resisting Miss Merryweather / Emily Larkin. -- 1st ed.

ISBN 978-0-9941384-3-9

Dear Reader

Resisting Miss Merryweather is the second book in the Baleful Godmother series. A full list of the books in the series can be found at www.emilylarkin.com/books.

Those of you who like to start a series at the very, very, very beginning may wish to read the Fey Quartet novellas, where any questions you might have about *how* and *why* this particular family of women have a Faerie godmother are answered.

I'm currently giving away free digital copies of *The Fey Quartet* and *Unmasking Miss Appleby*, the first novel in the Baleful Godmother series, to anyone who joins my Readers' Group. If you'd like to claim your copies, please visit www.emilylarkin.com/starter-library.

Happy reading,

Emily Larkin

It is a truth universally acknowledged,

that Faerie godmothers do not exist.

CHAPTER ONE

April 6ᵗʰ, 1807
Devonshire

BARNABY WARE LET the curricle slow to a halt. He gazed past the horses' ears at the high-banked Devon lane that opened like a tunnel on his left. The knot of dread that had been sitting in his belly all morning tied itself even tighter. *Picturesque,* a voice noted in his head. The tall banks were clothed in grass and wildflowers and shaded by overhanging trees.

"This'll be the lane to Woodhuish Abbey, sir," his groom, Catton, said, with a nod at the lightning-struck oak on the far bank.

I know. But Barnaby didn't lift the reins, didn't urge the horses into motion.

Four days it had taken to get here, each day traveling more slowly. Today, he'd practically let the horses walk. And now, with less than a mile left of his journey, all he wanted to do was turn the curricle around and head back to Berkshire.

"No mistaking that oak," Catton said, after a moment's silence. "Split right in half, just like the innkeeper said."

I know. The dread was expanding in his belly, and growing apace with it was a bone-deep certainty that he shouldn't be here. So what if the invitation had been in Marcus's handwriting? *I shouldn't have come.*

Barnaby glanced over his shoulder. The road was empty. And there was plenty of space to turn the curricle.

Catton would think him a coward, but what did he care what the groom thought? What did he care what *anyone* thought anymore?

"Sir Barnaby Ware?" a female voice said.

Barnaby's head snapped around. He searched the shadows and found a young girl in a dark-colored redingote, up on the nearest bank, in the deep green gloom of the trees.

"Er . . . hello?" he said.

The girl descended the bank nimbly. She wore sturdy kid leather boots and a straw bonnet tied under her chin with a bow. How old was she? Twelve? Fourteen?

"Sir Barnaby Ware?" she asked again, stepping up to the curricle and tilting her head back to look at him.

Sunlight fell on her face, showing him sky-blue eyes and flaxen ringlets.

Barnaby blinked. Not a girl; a woman in her twenties, trim and petite. "Yes."

Was this Marcus's new wife? Surely not. The gossip was that the new Lady Cosgrove was a plain woman, and this woman was definitely not plain.

"I'm Anne Merryweather," the woman said, with a friendly smile. "Lady Cosgrove's cousin. May I possibly beg a ride to the abbey?"

"Of course," Barnaby said automatically, and then his brain caught up with his mouth. *Damnation*. He managed a stiff smile. "It would be my pleasure, Miss, er, Mrs.—?"

"Miss Merryweather," she said cheerfully. "But most people call me Merry. It's less of a mouthful!"

Half a minute later, Miss Merryweather was seated alongside him and Catton was perched behind in the tiger's seat. Barnaby reluctantly lifted the reins. It appeared he was going to face

Marcus after all.

His stomach clenched as they entered the shady lane.

"I saw you once at Vauxhall," Miss Merryweather said. "Several years ago."

Barnaby wrenched his thoughts back to his companion. "Er . . . you did?"

"At one of the ridottos."

Barnaby looked more closely at her—the heart-shaped face, the dimples, the full, sweet mouth. Did she expect him to recognize her? "I'm afraid I don't recall meeting you," he said apologetically.

"Oh, we weren't introduced. I was there with my fiancé, and you were with Lord Cosgrove and his fiancée."

"Oh." His face stiffened. The familiar emotions surged through him: guilt, shame, remorse.

Barnaby looked away, and gripped the reins tightly. God, to be able to go back to the person he'd been then. To be able to relive his life and not make the same dreadful mistake.

"I noticed you most particularly. You were the best dancer there."

It took a few seconds for the words to penetrate the fog of shame and regret. When they did, Barnaby blinked. "Me?"

"Marcus dances fairly well," Miss Merryweather said. "He's a natural athlete, but he's a pugilist. He's trained his body for strength, not grace. You, I'd hazard a guess, are a better fencer and horseman than Marcus."

"Not by much," Barnaby said, staring at her. What an unusual female.

"It takes a number of qualities to make a truly excellent dancer. Not merely precision and grace and stamina, but a musical ear as well, and of course one must *enjoy* dancing. You have all of those qualities, Sir Barnaby. You're one of the best dancers I've ever seen."

Barnaby felt himself blush. "Thank you." He refrained from glancing back at Catton. The groom was doubtless smirking.

"Marcus's neighbors are holding a ball tomorrow night. I know it's terribly forward of me, but I hope we can dance at least one set together?"

"Of course." And then he remembered Marcus. The blush drained from Barnaby's face. Dread congealed in his belly. "If I'm still here."

Miss Merryweather's eyebrows lifted slightly. "You're staying for two weeks, aren't you?"

"Perhaps not." Perhaps not even one night. It depended on Marcus. Depended on whether Marcus could bear to be in the same room as him. Could bear to even look at him.

Barnaby's stomach twisted in on itself. *This is a mistake. I shouldn't have come.* Some errors could never be atoned for. His hands tightened on the reins. The horses obediently slowed.

"Marcus expects you to stay for a fortnight, you know. He's been looking forward to your visit."

Barnaby felt even sicker. He glanced at Miss Merryweather. Her gaze was astonishingly astute. *Oh, God, how much does she know?*

He halted the curricle. "Miss Merryweather, I—"

She laid her gloved hand on his arm, cutting off his words. "Don't make any decisions now, Sir Barnaby. Wait until you've talked with Marcus."

She knows I'm about to turn around and run.

Miss Merryweather removed her hand and gave him a warm, sympathetic smile. "He says you're his best friend."

To Barnaby's horror, the words brought a rush of moisture to his eyes. He turned his head away and blinked fiercely, flicked the reins, urged the horses into a brisk trot. He concentrated on the shade-dappled lane, on the horses, on the reins, on his breathing—anything but Miss Merryweather's words.

The lane swung right, the grassy banks lowered, and a view opened out: woodland, meadow, a sweeping drive leading to a large stone building that must be Woodhuish Abbey. The abbey was a sprawling, whimsical structure, with gracefully arched windows and a crenellated roof parapet. Ivy climbed the stone walls.

"Beautiful, isn't it?" Miss Merryweather said.

Barnaby's brain was frozen in a state between dismay and panic. It took him several seconds to find a response. "Very gothic."

The curricle swung into the driveway. Gravel crunched beneath the wheels. Dread climbed his throat like bile. *Oh, God, I can't face Marcus again.* The last time had almost crucified him. But it was too late to turn back now. Far too late. They were within sight of the windows. Another minute and they'd be in front of the great, arched doorway.

Barnaby sat in numb horror while the horses trotted down the driveway.

"It was a monastery for more than three hundred years—Augustinian—they built the most *marvelous* walled gardens—but it's been in private hands since Henry the Eighth. Marcus says the previous owner remodeled it in the Strawberry Hill style. Are you familiar with Strawberry Hill, Sir Barnaby?"

Barnaby managed to unstick his tongue. "Walpole's place. Gothic."

He brought the curricle to a halt at the foot of the steps. Catton leapt down and ran to the horses' heads.

"Thank you for the ride, Sir Barnaby," Miss Merryweather said.

Barnaby's throat was too dry for a response. He managed a stiff nod. His fingers didn't want to release the reins.

The door swung open. A butler emerged into the sunlight. Behind him was another man, taller, younger, darker. Marcus.

Barnaby's stomach folded in on itself. *Oh, God.*

CHAPTER TWO

MERRY JUMPED LIGHTLY down from the curricle. Sir Barnaby appeared to have forgotten her existence. He was sitting as stiffly as a statue, watching Lord Cosgrove come down the steps, and the expression on his face . . .

Shame. Despair.

Merry looked quickly away, and up at the earl. Marcus's face was masklike, but she'd lived in his household for ten months now, and she knew him well enough to see his painful hope.

She smiled up at him. "I met Sir Barnaby at the end of the lane. He was kind enough to give me a ride."

Marcus nodded, and halted on the final step. Merry heard the front door open again, heard quick, light footsteps. Charlotte. She allowed herself to relax slightly. Marcus seemed to relax slightly, too. He glanced back, and held out a hand to his wife.

Lady Cosgrove came swiftly down the steps. She was smiling, but beneath the smile she was anxious. She took her husband's hand, glanced at Merry, and then at Sir Barnaby.

Sir Barnaby climbed down from the curricle. He had mastered his expression. His face was as masklike as Marcus's.

The groom cast a nervous glance between Sir Barnaby and Lord Cosgrove; he'd know the history between the two men.

For a moment they made a silent tableau, and then Marcus said, "Barnaby. Welcome to Woodhuish Abbey."

Sir Barnaby gave a jerky nod. His face was pale beneath the curling red-brown hair. "Thank you."

"I'd like you to meet my wife. Charlotte."

Sir Barnaby bowed. "It's a pleasure to meet you, Lady Cosgrove."

"And you, Sir Barnaby," Charlotte said, with a warm smile. She held out her hand to him.

After a moment's hesitation, Sir Barnaby took it.

"I'm so glad you could come."

Charlotte's sincerity was audible in her voice, but Sir Barnaby didn't appear to hear it. He gave another jerky nod, and released Charlotte's hand and took a step back, as if to put distance between them. "Thank you for your invitation. I'm . . . pleased to be here."

Merry almost snorted at this patent lie. *He wants to be anywhere but at Woodhuish. He'd be on his way back to Berkshire if I hadn't met him in the lane.*

"The stables are around the back," Marcus told the groom. "Come inside, Barnaby."

Sir Barnaby seemed to rock back slightly on his heels. He inhaled a shallow breath. He was painfully tense, and beneath the tension was wariness. He was bracing himself for . . . what? Recriminations?

They climbed the steps in a stiff, awkward gaggle. Merry watched Sir Barnaby as he stepped beneath the pointed gothic arch of the great door. He seemed to draw even more closely into himself.

Their footsteps echoed on the polished flagstone floor. The butler closed the huge door and stood silently, as poker-faced as only a butler could be.

"Are you hungry?" Marcus asked. "Would you like some refreshments?"

"No, thank you." Sir Barnaby glanced around the entrance

hall, his gaze skipping over the iron-bound oak chests that were each six hundred years old and the great curving staircase with its traceried stonework.

"I thought . . . perhaps you might like to go for a walk? I could show you Woodhuish. If you would like?" The invitation was diffidently extended, but Merry saw how anxiously Marcus waited for the response.

Sir Barnaby hesitated, and then nodded.

"In fifteen minutes?"

Sir Barnaby nodded again.

Marcus seemed to relax. "Good," he said. "I'll meet you down here. Yeldham will show you to your room."

The butler stepped forward. "If you would come with me, Sir Barnaby."

MERRY FOLLOWED MARCUS and Charlotte into the front parlor, with its tall French windows and view of the park. She peeled her gloves off thoughtfully and removed her bonnet. She had never before witnessed such a painful, awkward meeting between two people.

Charlotte took a seat by the windows, where sunlight fell across her lap. Marcus sat beside her and fidgeted, shuffling through the books on the side table, stacking them in a pile, glancing at the clock on the mantelpiece, restacking the books. The sixth time he looked at the clock, he said, "I, uh, I should go."

Charlotte touched his cheek with her fingertips, and then leaned over and kissed him. "I hope it goes well, love."

Marcus gave a brief nod, as jerky as Sir Barnaby's. He tugged at his neckcloth as if it were too tight and headed for the door.

When he had gone, Charlotte met Merry's eyes. "I've never

seen him so nervous."

Faintly, came the sound of men's voices, the sound of the great front door closing. Charlotte tilted her head, listening, and then said, "What do you think of Sir Barnaby?"

"He doesn't want to be here. He almost turned around at the end of the lane." Merry spread her gloves on her knee and smoothed out the limp fingers.

"I'm not surprised. Marcus said the most dreadful things to him the last time they met. Sir Barnaby practically begged for a second chance, and Marcus refused." Charlotte's lips twisted. "I've never seen a man look so stricken. I thought he was going to cry."

I saw that look on his face only a few minutes ago. Merry nodded soberly. "I think he's been even more damaged by this than Marcus. And I don't mean his reputation."

Outside, on the lawn, movement caught her eye. Marcus and Sir Barnaby came into view. Merry had seen hundreds of men walk into her father's dancing studio, but none had looked as uncomfortable as Sir Barnaby did now. He held himself stiffly, tensely, as if trying not to hunch in on himself.

Marcus was tense, too, but his was an eager, hopeful tension. He was half-turned to Sir Barnaby, talking, gesturing towards the abbey.

Sir Barnaby listened with his head slightly lowered, slightly averted.

He can't bring himself to meet Marcus's eyes.

"They're talking," Charlotte said, a note of hope in her voice.

"Hmm," Merry said. The difference between the man she'd seen dance at Vauxhall four years ago and the man now crossing the lawn was stark.

Her noncommittal response brought Charlotte's head around. "What do you see?"

A man who has built a dungeon for himself at the bottom of a deep, dark pit.

"I think . . . Sir Barnaby no longer believes that reconciliation is possible."

CHAPTER THREE

THEY CLIMBED A wooded hillside, and emerged into a cliff-top meadow. Rugged gray cliffs stretched north and south. To the east, the sea glittered blue and silver. *Is it my turn to say something?* Barnaby groped for a comment. "Beautiful."

A track ran near the edge of the cliff. "The riding officer's path," Marcus said. "You can look down into all the coves."

"Are there smugglers here?"

"Not here. Further north."

The stilted, awkward conversation dwindled into silence. They walked without talking. Butterflies fluttered among the wildflowers. A brisk breeze brought the scent of the ocean. Birds soared on the thermals, making sounds like cats mewing, and beneath those sounds, a voice echoed in his ears. Marcus's voice. *You fucked my wife.*

"I never thought you'd move so far from London," Barnaby said, when he couldn't bear the voice in his head any longer. "I always thought you'd stay within a day's ride of Parliament— and Jackson's."

"I'm stepping back from politics."

He glanced at Marcus in surprise. "You?" His gaze met Marcus's for a moment, before skidding sideways.

"The slave trade's abolished. And I have a son, now. I want to spend as much time with my family as I can. I don't intend to model myself on my father; my children are going to *know* me. And as for Jackson . . . I've hired one of his men as a groom, chap called Sawyer. He can't fight in the ring anymore—but he's good with horses. We spar several times a week. Sawyer usually wins. Charlotte says it's good for my vanity." Marcus grunted a laugh.

Barnaby's answering smile felt like a grimace. He looked away. *This is futile. We can't go back to what we once had.* It was impossible to mend something this broken.

"I had this seat built for Charlotte," Marcus said. "Towards the end of her pregnancy, she couldn't walk far, but she liked to come up here."

Barnaby glanced around.

The seat in question was wooden, solid and sturdy and big enough for two people. It faced the sea.

Marcus crossed to it and sat. After a moment's hesitation, Barnaby followed. His joints didn't want to bend; he sat as stiffly as an old man.

"I spent a lot of time here with Charlotte, that last month of her pregnancy," Marcus said, leaning his elbows on his knees. "It was cold. December."

Barnaby managed another smile-grimace. He looked down at his gloved hands. *I can't stomach two weeks of this, both of us pretending.*

"Marcus, this isn't going to work," he said quietly. "I'll leave tomorrow."

There was a long moment of silence, and then Marcus said, equally quietly, "I wish you wouldn't."

Barnaby closed his eyes. "Marcus—"

"You never told me what happened with Lavinia."

His brain rejected the words—*No, Marcus didn't just say that*—but his ears told him otherwise. Marcus *had* said it.

Barnaby's chest seemed to grow hollow with horror. Finally,

he turned his head and looked at Marcus. "You want to know?"

Marcus nodded.

I owe him that.

Barnaby looked down at his clenched hands. "She came to me one afternoon, asked to speak with me. We went for a walk in the gardens. When we got to the folly, she started crying, and she said that you'd taken to hitting her and that she was scared and . . . and I tried to comfort her, and . . . we had sex."

His mouth filled with excuses: *I never meant to. I don't know how it happened. I didn't plan to cuckold you.* Barnaby gripped his hands more tightly. "The next day, she came to see me again, and I told her we couldn't—and she cried, and when I wouldn't touch her, she flew into a rage. She . . ." He paused. How to put that alarming fury into words?

"I am familiar with Lavinia's tantrums," Marcus said dryly. "She broke things, threw things, screamed like a banshee."

Barnaby nodded, still looking at his hands. "And then she went back to Hazelbrook and told you what had happened between us."

Marcus stretched out his legs. "Actually, what Lavinia told me was that the two of you had been having an affair for several months."

Barnaby jerked his head around to stare at him, aghast. "What? No! It was only once!"

"And she also said that you seduced her."

Barnaby shook his head, open-mouthed, mute with disbelief.

"Lavinia was an excellent liar. I didn't realize *how* excellent until after her death." Marcus rubbed his brow. "So, she didn't start crying until you were at the folly?"

Barnaby closed his mouth, and shook his head again.

"A good choice of location. Secluded. Private. That handy chaise longue."

Barnaby felt himself flush. "I didn't choose to walk in that direction!"

"No, Lavinia chose. And she kissed you first, didn't she?"

Barnaby hesitated, and nodded.

"And initiated the sex?"

He nodded again.

"Tears and kisses, and then sex . . ." Marcus grimaced. "I fell for that ploy quite a number of times. I'd be astonished if *any* man could have resisted that one. She was exceptionally good at it."

Barnaby blinked. "What?"

"When it came to sex, Lavinia was a manipulator *par excellence*. She led me by my cock that first year of our marriage—and I was too blindly in love to notice. Even when I began to have my doubts, it took me months to acknowledge it. I didn't want to admit that she'd married me for my money and my title—because she was so damned *beautiful*."

Barnaby looked back down at his hands. Beautiful was too mild a word for the late countess. She had been luminous, slender and golden, as lovely as an angel.

"Lavinia used me. And when I stopped letting her walk all over me, she turned around and used *you,* too. You were a pawn, Bee. She seduced you in order to hurt me."

Barnaby pinched his thumbs together. *You think I haven't realized that?*

"My first memories are of you, you know?" Marcus said. "In fact, every good memory I have from my childhood has you in it."

Barnaby closed his eyes. He wished he could close his ears, too.

"Thirty *years,* Bee. We can't just let that go."

Barnaby opened his eyes and swallowed the lump in his throat. "It's over, Marcus. We can't go back."

"No. But we can go forward."

Can we? Can we bury a betrayal of that magnitude and carry on as if it never happened? He'd hoped so, once, but he knew better now. Barnaby shook his head.

There was a moment's silence, and then Marcus said, "Do you still believe I hit her?"

"No."

"And I *know* you didn't seduce her."

Barnaby unclenched his hands. "Doesn't matter who seduced whom, does it? I still had sex with your wife. I'm not someone who should be your friend."

"Bollocks."

Barnaby glanced at him and then away. "You don't trust me. You said so yourself, the last time—"

"That was a year and a half ago, Bee. I've changed my mind."

Barnaby stared down at the ground, at the grass, the wildflowers. An orange and brown butterfly settled on a nodding white comfrey head. "It's not the sort of thing you change your mind about."

"I won't say it came easily," Marcus said. "Because it didn't—I must have talked it over with Charlotte a hundred times—but the thing is, Bee, when I compared what you said that day at Mead Hall to what Lavinia had told me, I realized that she'd been lying and you'd been telling the truth, and that it *had* only been one afternoon—and if it was only the once . . . That changed things."

Barnaby stared down at the orange and brown butterfly.

"When Charles was born, when I saw him the first time—" Marcus paused. When he spoke again, his voice was lower: "If I were to die, and if for any reason Charlotte needed help . . . I hope she'd come to you. Because I know you'd look after her, and I know you'd look after my son. I've told Charlotte that. She knows it."

Barnaby's throat tightened. He watched the butterfly explore the flower head.

Half a minute slowly passed, and then Marcus asked, "Am I wrong to trust you?"

Barnaby shook his head. *I would die rather than betray you again.* "No."

Another half minute passed.

"What, then?" Marcus asked, an edge of frustration in his voice.

Barnaby blew out a breath, and turned his head to look at him. "For Christ's sake, Marcus. I had sex with your *wife*."

"So?"

"So, we can't be friends after that!"

"The last time I saw you, you asked if we could—"

"Well, I was wrong," Barnaby said flatly. "Some things are unpardonable, and what I did was one of them."

Marcus looked at him for a long moment, his gaze penetrating. "You can't forgive yourself."

Barnaby grimaced, and turned his head away. He'd cuckolded his *best friend*. How could any man who'd done that forgive himself?

The silence between them stretched. Barnaby stared down at the butterfly and listened to the waves crashing and the birds crying and the grass rustling in the breeze.

"I don't think there's a man in England who could have withstood Lavinia once she set her sights on him," Marcus said.

Barnaby had a flash of memory: Lavinia, her eyes starry with tears, her mouth tragic, begging him to kiss her. "A true friend would have—"

"Only if he was a eunuch."

Barnaby shook his head.

"You turned her away the second time, Bee. That counts for a lot. Believe me, I know *exactly* how much willpower it took to resist Lavinia."

Not willpower; shame. I was so sick with shame I couldn't even look at her.

Marcus sighed again. "If you wish to leave tomorrow, then of course you may. But I hope you'll stay." He paused, and then said, "We can't go back, Bee, but we can start again."

Barnaby closed his eyes. Start again? God, if only he *could* start again. Not be the man who had betrayed his best friend.

Too late. He would always be that man.

Marcus cleared his throat. His voice became diffident: "Charles is being christened next week. Charlotte and I were hoping that you'd stand as his godfather."

Barnaby's head jerked around. "Godfather?" he said, appalled. "Me?"

"Yes."

"But . . ." *But I cuckolded you. I can't stand as godfather to your heir.* Barnaby's throat was too tight for speech. He shook his head.

"Please think about it." Marcus pushed to his feet and stood for a long moment, looking down at Barnaby, his face unsmiling, his gray eyes serious. "He's called Charles after Charlotte's father, but his second name is Barnaby."

CHAPTER FOUR

MERRY LOVED THE cliff-tops. There was no better place for thinking; the breeze blew all the clutter out of one's head, and the view stretched forever, and there was something about the sea—the constant, rhythmic swell, the sharp salt-tang, the thud-crash of waves against the cliffs—that was both invigorating and calming.

This afternoon, Merry had a lot to think about. Sir Barnaby's arrival, most especially. She strode along the cliffs to her favorite spot, where gray limestone thrust up out of the grass, weathered into fantastical shapes by centuries of wind and rain. Here was the patch of the grass where she liked to sit, the rock she liked to lean her back against, and the view she liked to gaze at, out over the sea.

Merry intended to bend her mind to the problem of Marcus and Sir Barnaby, but she found herself fishing her mother's letter out of her pocket by habit. The corners were tattered and the creases almost worn through.

My darling Anne,

If you are reading this letter, it is because I am dead, and dead or not, there is something very important I must tell you. It is this: You have a Faerie godmother.

How absurd it sounds! I know I thought it a great joke, when your grandmother told me. However, as I have recently discov-

ered, it is no joke, but the perfect truth.

On your twenty-fifth birthday, you will be visited by a Faerie. Treat her with utmost caution. She is a malicious creature who delights in doing harm. No one knows her true name, but among our family, she is known as Baletongue.

Baletongue will offer you a Faerie gift. Choose very carefully, my love. The wrong choice can lead to madness or death. I am enclosing a list of the gifts you may choose from. Your grandmother received it from her mother. Read the annotations thoroughly.

The list her mother referred to was safely locked in Merry's escritoire. She could see it in her mind's eye: the old parchment, the fading ink.

There were so many tempting choices—the one Charlotte had chosen, for example: metamorphosis. Who wouldn't want to be able to turn into a bird and fly? But the gift she kept coming back to, time and time again, was *Finding People and/or Objects*. According to the annotations, two of her ancestresses had chosen it.

Merry narrowed her eyes and stared out at the white-capped sea. All she needed was to find one hoard of treasure, and she'd have enough money to buy a town house in Bath or London, or a pretty cottage in the country, or perhaps even both.

Is that the gift I want?

Five days left to decide, and she still didn't know. Merry blew out her breath. She refolded the letter, placed it in her pocket, and bent her mind firmly to the problem of Marcus and Sir Barnaby.

It was a problem with two halves. One: Marcus. Two: Sir Barnaby.

She knew Marcus's character, knew his values, knew how his mind worked. Sir Barnaby Ware was a mystery.

Therefore, I need to understand what's going on inside his head.

Merry climbed to her feet and continued along the path, her stride purposeful. The rest of the afternoon laid itself out neatly in her head: she'd walk along the cliffs, then run Sir Barnaby to ground and offer to show him the walled gardens.

She could surely unravel the workings of Sir Barnaby's mind in an hour spent among the espaliered trees and beds of vegetables. It was merely a matter of introducing the right topics and watching his reactions.

At this point, her plan underwent an abrupt change, for there, sitting on Charlotte's cliff-top seat, was Sir Barnaby Ware. Alone.

Merry's steps slowed. Sir Barnaby sat with his elbows on his knees, his posture so weary, so sad, that it hurt to look at him.

She felt an almost overwhelming urge to hug him tightly, as if he were a child and not a grown man. But hugs weren't going to mend *this* problem.

"Hello!" Merry called, when she was a dozen yards away. The wind snatched her voice from her mouth and flung it ahead of her.

Sir Barnaby stood before she reached him. "Miss Merryweather," he said courteously.

"What do you think? Isn't it beautiful?" It was easy to let her enthusiasm spill over. She loved these cliffs.

Sir Barnaby's answering smile was mechanical. "Very beautiful."

"Did Marcus take you as far as Woodhuish House? No? Well, I'm heading that way. You must come with me!"

She saw reluctance in his infinitesimal hesitation and in the flicker of his eyelids. *He wants to be alone.* But Sir Barnaby was too polite to say so aloud. "It would be my pleasure," he said.

They walked side by side along the riding officer's path. Sir Barnaby made a good pretense of strolling—he commented on the wildflowers, the limestone cliffs, the seabirds—but it was obvious that most of his attention was turned inward.

If she was to gain any understanding of him, she needed to see the real Sir Barnaby, not this polite automaton walking alongside her.

"I wonder if you ever met my father, Sir Barnaby?" Merry said, watching his face closely. "He was a dancing master. Alexander Merryweather."

She saw the blink of surprise, the slight blankness of his face as he processed the words, the dawning realization in his raised eyebrows. "You're Alexander Merryweather's daughter?"

"Yes."

That had broken through his preoccupation. Sir Barnaby halted, and stared at her in astonishment. Merry stared back intently. The next few seconds would tell her about his sense of self-importance.

The change from politeness to polite condescension was sometimes overt, sometimes almost imperceptible, but Sir Barnaby displayed none of the signs. He didn't draw away from her. His chin didn't lift; it lowered. And it wasn't haughtiness in his eyes, but interest.

Not a snob.

"I never met him, but I *heard* of him, of course. He was legendary." And then Sir Barnaby's manner altered again. There was genuine sympathy in his eyes, in his voice. "I heard he died last year. I'm very sorry, Miss Merryweather."

Merry nodded acknowledgment of his sympathy. "Thank you."

She saw an unspoken question form on Sir Barnaby's face, and then his expression became politely disinterested. He resumed strolling.

Merry matched her steps to his. What had he been about to ask? *Why am I at Woodhuish Abbey?* "After Father's death, I went to live with friends of his, but then Charlotte and I became acquainted—our relationship is *very* distant, neither of us knew the other existed! And she kindly invited me to live with her." Charlotte had been researching her ancestry, trying to find others who shared the same Faerie godmother—but *that* wasn't a detail she could share with Sir Barnaby.

"Your mother's family didn't take you in?" he said neutrally. "Your grandfather's Lord Littlewood, is he not?"

"My mother's family doesn't acknowledge my existence."

Sir Barnaby uttered a faint snort. "The Littlewoods have always been very high in the instep. One would take Littlewood for a duke, the way he carries on." And then he glanced sideways at her and gave a wry, self-deprecating smile. "Says a lowly baronet."

Merry smiled back. *I like this man.* "At least they're consistent. They never acknowledged Mother after her marriage. They'd have looked foolish, if they'd suddenly turned around and acknowledged *me*."

"Heaven forbid that a Littlewood should ever look foolish," Sir Barnaby said, dryly. The sea breeze blew the hair back from his brow. He had a very pleasant face, Merry decided. His features were harmoniously arranged, and more than that, his *colors* were harmonious—the red-brown hair, the hazel eyes, the light tan, the freckles. If autumn were personified, he would be Sir Barnaby.

There were laughter lines at his eyes and mouth, but she didn't think Sir Barnaby had laughed in a long time. A resolution formed between one step and the next: *I shall make him laugh today.*

"The Bromptons' ball promises to be well-attended," Merry said. "I expect at least a dozen couples will stand up."

The latent humor vanished from Sir Barnaby's face. "I won't be attending the ball."

"You're leaving tomorrow?"

Mixed emotions crossed Sir Barnaby's face. She saw that he wanted to leave—and that he felt he couldn't. "I haven't yet decided."

"Well, if you *do* stay, we shall stand up for the minuet and a country dance. Agreed?"

Sir Barnaby's lips compressed. "I stopped dancing several years ago."

His tone, his expression, told her that he'd stepped back into his self-imposed dungeon.

"Nonsense," Merry said, cheerfully. "The minuet and a country dance. Agreed?" She halted and held out her hand to him.

Sir Barnaby halted, too. He looked at her, a frown pinching between his eyebrows, his lips pressed together, reluctance writ clear on his face.

Merry almost backed down—and then she remembered the Sir Barnaby she'd seen at Vauxhall, remembered his blatant joy in dancing. This was a man who *needed* to dance, whether he realized it or not. She kept her hand held out and an expectant smile on her face, and waited, counting the seconds in her head. *Five, six, seven.*

"The minuet and a country dance," Sir Barnaby said, finally. "If I stay."

They shook hands. "Agreed."

Sir Barnaby repossessed his hand. He had the expression of a man girding himself for an ordeal: dismayed, and trying not to show it. Merry almost apologized. It hadn't been polite of her to push—had been extremely *im*polite in fact.

The path climbed steeply for several minutes. By the time they reached the highest point on the cliffs, Sir Barnaby had mastered his dismay and acquired his blankly courteous look again. Merry ransacked the corners of her brain for a topic that would make him forget his problems and allow her to see the underlying man again.

"My father excelled as a dancing master, not because he was a superb dancer—which he *was*—but because of his ability to read people."

Sir Barnaby glanced at her politely.

"You can learn a great deal about people by watching them for a few minutes. What do they look for when they first walk into a room? How do they interact with the other people there? Who do they acknowledge? Who do they ignore?"

Sir Barnaby's expression was still only politely attentive.

"Father taught me how to judge a person's character by observation. I often played the music for his lessons, you know. We'd make our own evaluations of the students' personalities, and compare them after the lesson."

A faint glimmer of interest showed in his eyes.

"It took me several years to master the trick. Father always saw so much more than I did. It was rather frustrating, for all that it was fascinating." She paused. *Say something, Sir Barnaby.*

"I can imagine it would be," Sir Barnaby said, and his expression told her that he *was* trying to imagine it.

"Father would tailor his lessons to suit his students; different methods work for different people. If he thought it would help someone, he'd have me partner them—but he was always extremely careful who he selected for me. And if he thought a student might become ill-mannered, he'd send me away before the lesson even started." She paused again. "Do you think the ill-mannered students were noblemen's sons, or tradesmen's sons?"

Sir Barnaby's eyebrows twitched faintly upwards. He thought for a moment, and then said. "Noblemen's sons."

Merry gave him an approving nod. "The tradesmen's sons were *always* courteous."

"And the gentlemen's sons?"

"On the whole, very civil. Although once we had a new stu-dent, a baronet's son, and Father sent me away within seconds of his entering the room. I gather he would have been quite *un-*civil, if I'd stayed."

Sir Barnaby's eyebrows lifted again. "Who was he?"

"You might know him. He'd be about your age. Sir Humph-rey Filton."

"Filton?" Emotions flickered across Sir Barnaby's face. Shock was predominant. He halted on the path. "Good God, I should *hope* your father sent you away!"

"Why?"

"Filton was . . . is . . ." Sir Barnaby acquired a faintly stuffed look. She'd seen it before on men's faces. It meant that the con-versation had taken a turn that was unsuitable for female ears.

"I *am* an adult," Merry reminded him. "I doubt that anything you say will shock me."

Sir Barnaby eyed her for a moment, and then said bluntly, "Filton was expelled from school for assaulting one of the maids. And then he was sent down from Oxford for doing the same thing."

"Oh." Merry mentally replaced *assaulting* with *raping*.

"I've seen Filton sober, and I've seen him drunk. He says the foulest things about women. He's . . ." Sir Barnaby frowned, selecting his words. "He's dangerous. He should be locked up."

"He's not?"

"His family has kept him out of the courts. They're extremely wealthy, and he's the only son."

They resumed walking. The wind tugged at Merry's bonnet. She gripped the brim firmly, and glanced at Sir Barnaby. Their conversation had taken a more serious turn than she'd intended, but it had effectively diverted him from his own problems. His attention was focused outwards.

"He'll go too far one day, Filton. He'll kill some poor woman—and hang for it. But it shouldn't have to come to that! He should have been stopped *years* ago. Money shouldn't be able to circumvent justice!"

He sounded so like Marcus that Merry almost blinked. "Are you active in politics, too?"

"Me? No." Sir Barnaby's face lost its animation. He looked away from her. After a moment, he said, "Marcus says he's giving up politics."

"Marcus will never give up politics. His sense of social justice is too strong."

"The slave trade act has passed—"

"Abolishing slavery isn't his only interest. Get him talking about the slums."

Sir Barnaby glanced at her.

"He's extremely passionate on the subject. It'll be his next crusade."

"Crusade?" Sir Barnaby's lips twitched briefly. "Yes, Marcus is a crusader." His expression was unguarded for an instant. She saw how much he respected Marcus, saw how deep his affection went—and then the shutters drew across his face again.

You are his current crusade, Sir Barnaby. Have you realized that?

She didn't think he had.

The path swung right, following the curve of the cliff. The wind was strong enough to make Merry's eyes water. Ahead was the long slope down to the cove. She glanced at Sir Barnaby. She'd learned a lot about him in the last ten minutes—his character, his values—but she hadn't come close to making him laugh.

Merry halted at the top of the slope. "When it's this windy, I usually run down here," she confessed.

Sir Barnaby's eyebrows rose. "Run?"

"It feels like flying." Merry spread her arms and leaned into the wind. "See?"

Sir Barnaby hesitated a few seconds, and then spread his arms. He had the expression of a man humoring a child—dubious, half-embarrassed.

"It's best when the wind's even stronger," Merry told him. "But this will do. Come on. It's fun."

She ran down the slope, her arms outstretched. The wind caught her with each stride and made her briefly buoyant. Laughter bubbled in her chest. *Maybe I should choose levitation as my Faerie gift.* Being able to fly—truly fly—would be incredible beyond anything.

Halfway down, Sir Barnaby passed her at a gallop, arms spread like wings, coattails flapping. Merry reached the bottom several seconds after him. He swung round to face her, his face alight with laughter.

Merry's pulse tripped over itself and sped up. She stared at Sir Barnaby, at his wind-tousled hair and laughing hazel eyes.

This is a man I could fall in love with.

CHAPTER FIVE

BARNABY SHOOK HIS head and grinned down at Miss Merryweather. "You are most definitely *not* a Littlewood."

As soon as the words were out of his mouth, he realized they could be misconstrued as an insult. But Miss Merryweather didn't take them as such. She grinned back at him, dimples springing to life in her cheeks, and retied her bonnet. "Thank you. I have no desire to be a Littlewood." The dimples vanished and her mouth pursed thoughtfully. "Apparently my grandfather thinks that laughter is vulgar. Mother said she used to be sent to her room for laughing. Sad, don't you think?"

"Yes."

"My father's philosophy was the exact opposite. He said it was important to laugh every day."

Laugh every day? There'd been a time when he'd done that. A lifetime ago, now. Barnaby raked a hand through his disheveled hair and glanced back up the long grassy slope. He must have looked ridiculous, running down that. A thirty-two-year-old child.

He had a deep longing to do it again.

Barnaby glanced at Miss Merryweather. She was watching him, her eyes astute. *She knows I want to run down again.*

Barnaby turned his back resolutely on the hillside. The route branched in front of them, one path hugging the rocky shore, one heading inland. "Where to now?"

Miss Merryweather gestured to the inland path.

For a moment, Barnaby almost balked. He wanted to keep walking the coastline, wanted to be the man who could laugh again, not the man who had to go back to Woodhuish Abbey and be Marcus's guest.

He took a deep breath, and released it in a sigh. The light-hearted, momentary joy drained away. The weight of his betrayal settled on him again. He matched his step to Miss Merryweather's.

The rough meadow became woodland, cool and green and dark, smelling of loamy soil and leaf mold. Barnaby's ears caught the sound of children's voices. He glanced to his left, up the wooded slope. Two boys, perhaps seven or eight years old, came hurrying through the undergrowth, their faces glowing with excitement. They pulled up short when they saw him and Miss Merryweather.

"Good afternoon, young Clem," Miss Merryweather said. "And young Harry. What mischief have you two been up to?"

Both boys grinned at her. "Nothing, miss," the taller of the two said. He had cobwebs in his hair, and carried a small shovel. The shorter boy had dirt smeared across his forehead.

Miss Merryweather put her hands on her hips. "Why don't I believe you?" she said, with mock severity.

The shorter boy gave her a sheepish grin, but the taller one managed a good expression of injured innocence.

Miss Merryweather laughed. "Away home with you. Your mothers will be wondering where you are."

They scampered past. Barnaby watched them run out of sight. *That was Marcus and me, twenty-five years ago.*

"I'd wager they've found a cave."

Barnaby glanced at her. "Cave?"

"This coast is riddled with them. There's a large one near

Torquay. Marcus took us to view it last year. I felt as if the roof was going to fall on my head the whole time." Miss Merryweather glanced up the wooded hillside. "I must remember to tell Marcus. If there *is* a cave, the men need to make sure it's safe."

If there is a cave, I wouldn't mind being in on that expedition.

They followed the boys along the path and emerged into open parkland. Ahead was a large manor house built of red brick. "Woodhuish House," Miss Merryweather said. "It's part of the estate."

"Who lives here?"

"No one yet. Marcus hasn't decided what to do with it."

Barnaby ran his eyes along the building, noting the oriel windows, the wide four-centered arches. "Tudor." His gaze took in the brick chimneys, tall and decorated with curvilinear patterns. Whimsical chimneys. *Fun* chimneys.

"Marcus says your home in Surrey was Tudor."

Barnaby nodded. "It was. But it was nothing like this." Mead Hall had been built of gray stone, its chimneys grimly unadorned.

"You sold it, I understand."

He nodded again.

"Why?"

Barnaby shrugged. "I didn't like it." He turned his face from her, pretending to admire the long view up the valley. *Didn't like?* Mead Hall had to be the place in England he hated the most. He hadn't been able to set foot in the garden since that afternoon with Lavinia, but he'd held on to Mead Hall for more than a year, stubbornly—stupidly—forcing himself to live there, hoping that Marcus would return to his estate next door, hoping they could patch things up between them.

And then one day Marcus *had* returned.

Barnaby's chest tightened in memory. Marcus's voice rang in

his ears. *You fucked my wife.*

He'd put Mead Hall on the market the very next day. It had been a relief to walk away from the place and know that he would never see it again.

"You live in Berkshire now, I understand. Do you like it there?"

"Yes." *It has no bad memories, and no one knows who I am.* "It's . . ." He searched for an adjective. "Quiet." Far from London and the barbed gossip of the *ton.*

Ahead, the valley stretched for half a mile of meadow and trees, with the abbey just visible in the distance. As views went, it was as picturesque as anything Gainsborough had painted, but Barnaby was unable to appreciate it. He walked alongside Miss Merryweather, his legs moving automatically while his brain chewed through the cliff-top conversation with Marcus. *Godfather? Me?*

He knew he had to decline. But how could he tell Marcus that without hurting him? It was impossible.

The abbey drew closer. Barnaby could see each arched window, see each crenellation on the parapet.

He discovered that he had halted.

Miss Merryweather halted, too. "You think you're the villain in this piece," she said, matter-of-factly. "But you're not."

It took a moment for the words to penetrate. *What* had she just said? Barnaby turned his head and frowned at her. "I beg your pardon?"

"I believe I have a fairly accurate understanding of what happened. Marcus told me before you arrived." Miss Merryweather's tone was faintly apologetic. "He didn't want me to judge you based on London gossip."

Was that sympathy in her eyes? Pity?

Barnaby found himself suddenly furiously angry. "He told you I was Lavinia's pawn, didn't he? Well, he's right. I was!

But what Marcus forgets is that I'm not a lump of ivory sitting helpless on a chessboard. I *knew* what I was doing!" Bitterness was harsh in his voice, corrosive on his tongue. "So don't tell me I'm not the villain in this piece, because I *am*."

Miss Merryweather was unfazed by his anger. "You're entitled to your opinion, of course, Sir Barnaby, but when *I* look at you, I don't see a villain. I see someone who made a colossal mistake for which he can't forgive himself. And I think that if you allowed yourself to be Marcus's friend again, you'd be an even better one than you were before. But that's just *my* opinion. You, of course, may disagree." Her gaze was cool, challenging.

Barnaby stared at her. He couldn't think of a single thing to say.

"You'll never do anything like that again, will you?"

I would rather die. He shook his head, mutely.

"So forgive yourself, and be an even better friend to Marcus than you were before."

Barnaby swallowed. "It's not as easy as that." He looked away from her, towards Woodhuish Abbey.

"No, I can see that."

Barnaby stared at the ivy-covered abbey. He knew he should start walking again, but he couldn't make his feet move. Half a minute passed. A minute passed. Finally, he blurted, "Marcus has asked me to stand as godfather to his son."

When Miss Merryweather made no response, he looked at her. She was watching him, her gaze shrewd and assessing.

"I can't do it. Think what people would say!"

"That you're friends again."

"There are . . . other interpretations that could be placed on it." The most obvious being that he'd cuckolded Marcus again, that his role as godfather was tacit acknowledgement that the child was his. Especially if the boy was christened Charles Barnaby.

"You're borrowing trouble. Charles has Marcus's coloring."

Barnaby looked down at the ground, and dug a lump of grass out with his heel. "He deserves a better godfather."

"Does he? That's a matter of opinion, surely?"

Barnaby glanced at her.

Miss Merryweather smiled, a warm smile that made dimples dance in her cheeks, and held out her hand. "Come inside. Meet little Charles. You don't have to decide today, you know."

CHAPTER SIX

MISS MERRYWEATHER'S WORDS stayed with Barnaby half the night, jostling for space in his head along with everything Marcus had said. His skull would surely burst soon, from the pressure of all that was crammed into it. Sleep came in snatches. He woke at dawn, weary and unrefreshed, to the quiet sounds of a housemaid laying a new fire in the grate. When she'd gone, Barnaby burrowed deeper into his bedclothes and tried to find unconsciousness again, but already thoughts were turning over in his head. It was like having a nest of writhing eels inside his skull. They wouldn't stop *moving*.

He closed his eyes, and slowed his breathing . . . and the eels in his head slid over one another and gave him Lavinia. Lavinia, sobbing in his arms. Lavinia pressing her warm, salty lips to his.

Memory unfolded: returning her kiss, unthinkingly and instinctively, wanting nothing more than to comfort her—and then jerking back when he realized what he was doing.

The eels in his head obligingly produced another memory: Lavinia's face—the starry, tear-filled eyes, the soft, vulnerable mouth. *Please kiss me, Barnaby,* she'd begged. *Please make me feel safe.*

And he had. God help him, he had. He'd gently kissed her mouth, her cheeks, her eyelids, gently kissed every inch of her exquisite face, and Lavinia had clung to him, and kissed him back, and sighed his name.

Somehow, gentle comfort had become passion and he'd found himself consumed by a fierce, overpowering tenderness. Their kisses had become more urgent. He hadn't noticed Lavinia opening his breeches—he'd been too lost in her mouth—but he'd sure as hell noticed her hand on his cock. He'd released her abruptly, jerking back as if scalded, cracking his head painfully against the wall.

Please, she'd whispered, tear-stained and achingly beautiful. *Please, Barnaby. I know you won't hurt me.* And tears had welled again in her eyes, and he'd been lost. Lost and doomed.

If he'd thought about it, he would have *known* that Marcus had never hit her. But he hadn't thought. He'd accepted her lies, had seen himself as her savior, her protector.

Lavinia had been the one to unfasten his breeches, but it had been *he* who'd gently pushed her gown up to her waist. He who had settled himself carefully between her thighs. He who had fucked her.

He'd wanted to protect, to comfort, to love—and instead he'd destroyed. Destroyed Marcus's marriage. Destroyed the most important friendship he'd ever had.

Lavinia had sighed and trembled in his arms, and clung to him, and whispered that she loved him, and in that moment, he'd loved her, too, so fiercely, so protectively, that if Marcus had walked into the folly, he'd probably have killed him.

But Marcus hadn't.

Once Lavinia had gone, the reality of what he'd done had sunk in. And on its heels had come shame. Shame, like ashes in his mouth. Shame so intense he'd almost vomited. He'd retreated to his study and got thoroughly drunk and he *had* vomited, had spent half the night vomiting. It had emptied his stomach, but done nothing for the shame.

"Fuck," Barnaby said, under his breath. He flung back the

bedclothes, padded barefoot to the window, and opened the shutters. Daylight flooded in. He leaned his hands on the windowsill and gazed out at Woodhuish and sighed.

What am I doing here?

Barnaby sighed again, and pushed away from the windowsill. He turned to the cheval mirror and looked at himself: red-brown hair standing on end, tired hazel eyes. That afternoon in the folly had turned him into someone he didn't recognize. *I don't know who I am anymore.*

He raked his hands through his hair and rang for hot water.

THE DAY LIMPED past. Marcus didn't inflict another excruciating *tête-à-tête* on him. Miss Merryweather didn't skewer him with her astuteness. Everyone was polite, friendly, tactful. He had a sense that Marcus and Lady Cosgrove and Miss Merryweather and even the servants were tiptoeing around him, waiting. Waiting for him to leave or stay or jump off the damned cliff.

Barnaby couldn't decide whether it was worse to be young Charles's godfather or not. Worse to stay or to go.

He rode as far as the River Dart with Marcus, ate luncheon at the abbey in the open gallery that had once been the monastery cloister, strolled the grounds with Lady Cosgrove and Miss Merryweather, and then suddenly dusk was drawing close, and he was in the entrance hall, waiting for the carriage to take them to the ball.

Barnaby fidgeted with his cuffs. *Why did I let Miss Merryweather talk me into this?* He felt like Robespierre headed for the guillotine. All that was missing was the tumbrel.

Marcus strolled down the stairs and took a moment to check his neckcloth in the mirror, adjusting the knot fractionally.

Barnaby scuffed one shoe on the polished flagstones. "Are you sure you want to be seen in public with me?" he said, in a low voice.

Marcus didn't look away from his neckcloth. "I'm not going to bother answering that."

Barnaby blew out a breath and tugged at his cuffs again.

Marcus turned away from the mirror. "I think you'll enjoy it," he said, leaning his shoulders against the wall. "Sir Anthony's interested in improving his land. I told him to talk to you. Sang your praises, actually."

Land improvement? Barnaby scuffed his other shoe on the flagstones. He could talk about land improvement for hours. Crop rotation. The new grasses. Animal husbandry. But it was hardly a topic for a dinner party.

A clatter of hooves came faintly from outside.

"The tumbrel's here," he said glumly.

Marcus laughed—and Barnaby found himself almost smiling back.

"It's not as bad as that." Marcus pushed away from the wall. "The Ances are nice people, and so are the Tuckney-Smythes. Ask Merry; she'll dissect their characters in detail for you. She has a very keen eye."

I'd noticed, Barnaby thought dryly, and then he said, "Miss Merryweather mentioned a fiancé yesterday. I'm guessing . . . he's dead?"

"Accident at sea, several years ago. He was in the navy. Merry did tell me his name. Henry . . . Henry Marlow. Lieutenant Henry Marlow."

Barnaby nodded.

Marcus glanced at the clock, and the staircase. "The Woottons should be there tonight, too. I can guarantee they'll be delighted to meet you. Five daughters."

Barnaby's head jerked back, as if he'd been slapped. "Jesus Christ, Marcus! You haven't been touting me as a bridegroom? I'm the last person any woman should marry!"

Marcus snorted. "If you believe that, you've got a maggot in your head." Then, his eyes narrowed. "You *do* believe it." He took a step towards Barnaby and lowered his voice and said fiercely, "For crying out loud, Bee, let it *go*." He shut his mouth and turned away as the butler bustled into the entrance hall, his shoes slapping briskly on the floor.

"The carriage is ready, sir."

"Thank you, Yeldham."

The countess and Miss Merryweather chose that moment to descend the stairs. A smile lit Marcus's face when he saw his wife. The countess wasn't pretty, but she was a very attractive woman, slim and elegant in a gown of amber silk shot with gold. Spectacles perched on her nose, and behind the lenses, her eyes were dark and intelligent. Barnaby thought, not for the first time today, that the gossips who'd labeled her plain must be blind.

The countess wasn't pretty, but Miss Merryweather most definitely was. Barnaby blinked, and took a second look at her. Flaxen ringlets, laughing eyes, dimples peeking in her cheeks. In that gown she was very definitely *not* a young girl. Short and slender, yes, but with a woman's breasts.

He tore his gaze from her, cleared his throat, and made his leg to both ladies.

Miss Merryweather crossed to him, almost bouncing on her toes. Her gown was the exact shade of blue as her eyes. "The minuet and a country dance. You promised."

"Indeed, I did."

That promise no longer seemed such a grave mistake.

CHAPTER SEVEN

MERRY KEPT A watchful eye on Sir Barnaby. He pokered up splendidly when they reached Brompton Court—she practically saw him don invisible armor as they climbed the steps to the front door—but when no sidelong glances or sly whispers came his way, he lost his stiff self-consciousness. Serendipity seated her across from him at the long, gleaming mahogany dinner table, and a fortunate gap in the flower arrangement afforded her a good view of him. During the first course she watched him gently and kindly draw out Sir Anthony's shyest daughter, seated on his right. When the second course arrived, he turned his attention to Sir Anthony's mother, stout in her widow's silks on his left. Sir Barnaby made the dowager laugh twice.

The meal drew to its close, the other guests arrived, the musicians tuned their instruments, and finally came the moment she'd been looking forward to for weeks: the ball.

"I believe this is the first of our dances," Sir Barnaby said, offering her his arm.

"It most definitely is."

Merry walked out onto the dance floor with him and inhaled a deep, joyful breath.

"I should warn you, it's been a while since I last danced," Sir Barnaby said diffidently. "I may forget some of the steps."

"You won't."

The musicians played the opening bars. Sir Barnaby bowed, Merry curtsied, and the minuet began.

Sir Barnaby danced just as she remembered. Not flashily, not showily, but with beautiful simplicity. He *was* slightly stiff to start with, but after the first dozen bars, his tension evaporated and he became the man she'd seen at Vauxhall. The man who danced as naturally as he breathed. He met her eyes and grinned.

Merry almost missed a step.

A voice whispered in her ear: *This man.*

A COUNTRY DANCE followed the minuet, and after that came a reel. Merry made her way through the figures, but her attention wasn't on the dancing. She felt almost dizzy with astonishment, with wonder.

Have I fallen in love with Sir Barnaby?

When Henry had died, she'd thought she could never love another man, but her heart was telling her she loved Sir Barnaby, and her head was telling her she loved him, and she knew— *knew*—it was true.

She had fallen in love with Sir Barnaby Ware.

The speed of it dazed her—she'd met him only yesterday— but her parents had fallen in love within an hour of meeting each other, and their love had lasted the rest of their lives. As her mother had said, sometimes you just *knew*.

Merry followed Sir Barnaby with her eyes. He'd clearly forgotten he was a villain. She watched him escort the eldest Wootton daughter onto the dance floor, watched him lead her through the steps, smiling, talking, making her laugh. The girl lost her anxious stiffness. By the end of the set, her *jeté assemblé* was almost graceful. Sir Barnaby returned her to her mother, and said something that made Mrs. Wootton look gratified and her daughter blush. The girl's gaze followed Sir Barnaby as he walked away. *Oh, dear, she's lost her heart to him.*

And why not? Sir Barnaby was every young country girl's dream. Wealthy, single, and if not a nobleman, the next best thing: a baronet. His face was attractive, his shoulders filled his coat admirably, his calves needed no padding—and most importantly of all, he was nice. Simply and genuinely *nice.*

Merry watched him approach. He was as tall as Marcus, but lankier. It was easy to see that he'd be a better swordsman than a pugilist.

Sir Barnaby halted in front of her. His hazel eyes were smiling. "Our country dance, Miss Merryweather."

Her heart squeezed in her chest. She found herself blushing as bashfully as Miss Wootton.

DANCING WITH A superb partner sometimes made Merry's blood hum. Tonight it wasn't just her blood that hummed; the marrow in her bones seemed to hum, too.

With Henry, she'd felt deeply comfortable. With Sir Barnaby, she felt not only comfortable, she felt *alive,* as if every part of her were conscious of him: blood, breath, bones. She felt alive—and at the same time, shy.

The shyness was disconcerting. Merry had danced with hundreds of men and never once felt shy, and yet tonight she did. So shy that she almost found herself tongue-tied.

They made their way down the set. Sir Barnaby held her gloved fingertips lightly. Merry was intensely aware of the warmth of his hand. *This man,* the voice repeated in her head, with utter certainty—and the emotions washed over her again: astonishment, joy, shyness.

She'd not been shy with Henry, but she'd felt the same certainty, and for the same reason: here was a man she could love forever. Not because of his face or his skill at dancing—

although those were certainly things she *liked* about Sir Barnaby—but because of who he was beneath those things: openminded and compassionate, patient and good-humored, a man who valued trust and loyalty highly.

A man who was struggling to forgive himself.

Merry stole a glance at Sir Barnaby. His hair gleamed in the light from the chandeliers, neither brown nor auburn, but something harmoniously in between.

He caught her glance and smiled, his eyes crinkling at the corners.

Merry's heart gave a loud thump. Shyness swept through her again, and with the shyness was certainty. *I want to spend the rest of my life with this man.*

CHAPTER EIGHT

BEFORE THE BALL, he'd had the notion that the carriage was a tumbrel and he was Robespierre headed for the guillotine; upon leaving the ball, Barnaby felt that he was the main character in Perrault's *Cendrillon*. When the clock struck midnight, the enchantment would be broken. The carriage would turn back into a pumpkin, the horses into mice, and he would revert to who he'd been before his godmother had cast her spell: a ragged cinder maid. Except that he didn't have a Faerie godmother, he wasn't female, and the rags and the cinders were of his own making.

Barnaby snorted under his breath. *Idiot.*

But the feeling of enchantment persisted in the warm, swaying darkness of the carriage. It felt as if the clock had turned back, as if that afternoon with Lavinia had never happened. Barnaby rested his head against the upholstery, stifled a yawn, and closed his eyes for a brief moment.

He woke with a jolt when the carriage arrived at Woodhuish Abbey. He blinked, sat up, and peered out the window. There were an uncommon number of servants waiting on the front steps. Not just the butler and three footmen, but the housekeeper too, and several men in the garb of stablemen and gardeners. Torches burned outside the great arched door, casting writhing shadows, turning human faces into gargoyle masks. The masks all had the same expression: desperately anxious. The housekeeper looked as if she'd been weeping.

Barnaby's tiredness evaporated instantly. *Something's wrong.*

Marcus jerked the carriage door open and jumped down, not waiting for a footman to let down the steps. "What's happened?"

"Two of the young boys are missing, sir," the butler said. "They didn't come home for their dinner."

"Which two?"

"Clem, sir," a gardener said. "And Harry." He was twisting his cloth cap in his hands, wringing it. Was he one of the boys' fathers? "We've searched the cliffs. Can't see nothing."

Miss Merryweather scrambled down from the carriage. "I think they found a cave. Over by Woodhuish House."

Marcus swung to face her. "You do? Why?"

"Sir Barnaby and I met them in the woods there, yesterday. Clem had a shovel."

"A cave?" The gardener's expression was torn between relief and fear. Was a son buried in a cave better than a son fallen off a cliff? *Yes, because the one in the cave may survive.*

"Can you show us where you saw them?" Marcus asked.

"We both can," Barnaby said.

Marcus turned back to the servants and gave rapid orders. Men ran to fetch shovels, ropes, lanterns. "Owens, saddle horses for us. Mrs. Thatcher, as many candles and tinderboxes as you can find, please. And some blankets." He turned to Lady Cosgrove and Miss Merryweather. "I know you'd like to help, but I ask you to stay here. If you can, sleep. There's no point in you staying awake all night."

"Are you certain I can't help?" the countess said, and there was an odd tone in her voice, as if her words were more than just a polite offer of assistance.

"I don't think so," Marcus said. "If I'm wrong, I'll send for you."

BARNABY FLUNG OFF his dress coat and skinned out of his satin knee breeches. He yanked on buckskins and boots, snatched up his riding gloves, and ran down to the stables, dragging on his Benjamin coat. Marcus joined him half a minute later. Men, shovels, ropes, lanterns, and blankets were loaded on to the hastily saddled horses. They rode up the valley at a canter. Barnaby counted ten servants, plus himself and Marcus, and his own groom, Catton. A pearly almost-full moon hung in the sky, casting enough light for him to see the hands of his pocket watch. Twenty to one.

They left the horses at Woodhuish House and entered the woods on foot. Beyond the reach of the lanterns, the shadows were ink-black.

The woods looked quite different in the dark. The trees seemed to crowd together, the shadows multiplying their branches. Barnaby was beginning to worry that he wouldn't recognize the spot, when he saw it. "I think it was here." He stepped off the path and held his lantern close to the ground, found scuff marks in the dirt. "Yes, here."

THEY CLIMBED THE hill slowly, laden with shovels and ropes, casting for a trail. The noise they made seemed huge in the darkness—undergrowth crackling and snapping, men panting, grunting. Shadows darted with each swing of the lanterns. "Here. Footprint," someone said.

Fifty yards further on, they found a narrow hole in the hillside. The hole was part natural, part chipped out by shovels. Fresh dirt lay scattered, and trodden into the dirt were child-sized boot prints.

"This is it," Marcus said, grim satisfaction in his voice.

The gardener with the cloth cap—Clem's father—thrust his

lantern into the hole. "Clem!" he shouted. "Harry!" His voice echoed hollowly.

No reply came.

It took two gardeners five minutes to widen the hole, chopping at the dirt with their shovels. The largest groom, the ex-pugilist Sawyer, levered out a limestone boulder the size of a small sheep, and heaved it aside. "That should do it, sir."

Marcus turned to his men. "No one goes inside without a lantern *and* spare candles *and* a tinderbox. Is that understood?"

A ragged chorus of "Yes, sir" came out of the darkness.

Barnaby shouldered his shovel, picked up his lantern, and followed Marcus into the hole.

The hole led to a rocky fissure, which in turn opened out into a cavern. Barnaby raised his lantern and looked around. Spires of rock pushed up from the floor and hung down from the ceiling, and behind the spires was darkness. His ears told him the cavern was huge.

"Christ almighty," he heard someone say in awe behind him.

One of the stablemen pushed past Barnaby. "Harry!" he bellowed.

The name echoed loudly, reverberating off walls and ceiling before slowly fading into silence. Barnaby watched the stableman's face, saw his hope, saw his anguish.

When the last of the echoes had died, Marcus spoke. "Penge, Farly, I know you're anxious about your boys, but we do this carefully. I don't want anyone getting hurt or lost." He waited until he'd seen the stableman nod. "We'll split in two, half go left, half go right, but *stay* in this cavern until we know how many exits there are. No one hares off on his own. Is that understood?"

THE CAVERN WAS smaller than a cathedral, but only just. It had three exits: the hillside hole, and two natural passageways, one broad, the other narrow. They split in half again to explore them. Barnaby led Catton, Clem's father, two gardeners, a stableman, and a footman down the narrower passageway.

It was more crevice than cave, shoulder-wide. The crevice kinked and twisted, the ceiling dropped so low that they had to duck their heads, then rose again, the passage widened slightly—and was blocked by a cave-in ahead.

Barnaby recalled Miss Merryweather's words. *I felt as if the roof was going to fall on my head.* "Stop," he said.

The men halted.

Barnaby raised his lantern and examined the ceiling before stepping closer to the debris.

The litter of boulders, stones, grit and dust looked fresh. He bent and picked up a fragment of rock. The broken surface was pale and clean, as if it had snapped off not an hour ago.

"Catton, go back and fetch the others, will you?" Barnaby kept his voice calm, aware of Clem's father at his shoulder. He unslung the rope he'd been carrying, tossed it aside, and examined the ceiling again. It *looked* safe. "Right, let's clear this."

CHAPTER NINE

SWEAT DRIPPED OFF Barnaby's face. There was grit in his eyes, grit in his mouth. He didn't speak, just panted, and all the time a silent prayer was running in his head. *Let them be alive.* He worked shoulder to shoulder with Marcus, digging with his hands, grabbing rocks, heaving them aside—and each time he reached into the rubble, he was afraid his groping hands would close on a bony ankle—and each time it was merely a rock, and his breath hitched with relief and he threw the rock aside and turned back to the debris—and felt the fear again.

"I'm through," cried a gardener who'd been working near the top of the cave-in.

Barnaby straightened, and wiped his face with a filthy sleeve.

Harry's father shoved past, scrambling over the rocks to the hole the gardener had made. It was no larger than a man's head, and as dark as an abyss.

"Harry?" he shouted. "Clem?"

Barnaby heard men panting all around him, and then he heard a faint cry like a bird. "Pa? Pa, is that you?"

"Harry! Are you all right? Is Clem with you?"

The voice came again, closer this time, louder. He heard how hard the boy was trying not to cry. "Clem broke his arm, Pa."

"Both alive," someone said. "Praise the Lord."

MARCUS LET PENGE and Farly speak to their sons, and then ordered everyone back. "We take it slowly from here, understood? Everyone's alive, and I want to keep it that way." He scanned the men's sweating, dusty faces. "Owens, take the carriage to Brixham and fetch Doctor Curnow to the abbey. You know where he lives? Howard, Arthur, go with him as far as the abbey and bring us back something to drink."

"Yes, sir!" The men hurried off.

Marcus scrambled up the rubble to the hole and raised his voice. "Harry, you and Clem stay well back. You hear me?"

"Yes, sir," came the faint reply.

THEY WIDENED THE hole slowly, passing rocks down from man to man, no longer driven by urgency, keeping a wary eye on the roof. Barnaby stripped down to his shirt and worked alongside Marcus again. If the servants had looked like gargoyles on the abbey steps, they looked like trolls now, filthy with dust and dirt.

When the two footmen returned laden with ale, they all took a break. Barnaby gulped his ale thirstily. The hoppy bitterness cleared his gritty mouth and stung his taste buds to life. He fished his watch out of his ruined waistcoat. Ten past four.

By four thirty, the hole was large enough for a man to crawl through. Five minutes later, both boys were out of their dark prison, white-faced and tearful and exhausted.

Barnaby found himself laughing with relief. He met Marcus's eyes and grinned.

Marcus grinned back. He'd never looked less like an earl. His hair stood on end, shaggy with dust, his face was plastered with sweat and grime, his shirt and breeches were filthy, his riding gloves torn, his boots ruined.

They gathered up shovels and ropes and blankets and lanterns and made their way out of the cavern, back to Woodhuish Abbey. Despite the early hour, the abbey was alive with light and bustle. Dr. Curnow had just arrived. They saw Clem into the doctor's care, and Harry into his mother's, and then all ate out in the stableyard on wooden benches, gardeners, stablemen, footmen, earl and baronet, shoulder to shoulder, wolfing down bread and cheese, draining tankards of ale.

After food came a hot bath, and then—as dawn lit the sky—bed. Barnaby fell asleep as abruptly and profoundly as if he'd swallowed a large dose of laudanum.

HE WOKE AT midday. For several minutes, he contemplated going back to sleep, then he levered himself out of bed, yawning, and wandered across to the window and opened the shutters. Sunlight streamed into the room, painting the colors in the carpet as bright as jewels.

Barnaby shaved and dressed and made his way downstairs. Servants brought him a late breakfast and a pot of tea in a parlor that looked out onto the cloister and its rose garden. "How's Clem's arm?" he asked a footman.

"Doctor splinted it. He says the boy will be fine, sir."

Barnaby was chewing his first mouthful when Miss Merryweather looked into the room. "You're awake. Excellent!" She drew out the chair opposite him and sat, her eyes eager. "Tell me it *all*. I've only heard it third-hand from one of the maids."

Barnaby told her while he ate his way through his plateful of eggs and sirloin. "It sounds as if the boys are extremely lucky to be alive," Miss Merryweather said, when he'd finished.

"They are." Barnaby reached for the teapot and poured himself another cup of tea, not because he wanted it, but because it gave him a reason not to look at Miss Merryweather. Her morning dress was plain cambric, her hair dressed in a simple knot, and yet somehow she managed to be even more captivating than she'd been last night—and he was *not* going to stare at her like a lovestruck schoolboy.

"I wish I'd remembered to tell Marcus on Monday."

He glanced at her and caught an expression on her face that gave him pause. He was not going to let her shoulder *that* guilt. "We both forgot."

"Yes." Miss Merryweather wrinkled her nose. "But at least we *did* meet them, otherwise no one would have known where to search." She shivered and rubbed her arms. "I don't like caves!"

Barnaby sipped his tea thoughtfully. "I think that cavern is the most extraordinary thing I've ever seen. I'd like to go back."

Her brow creased. "You would?"

Marcus chose that moment to enter the parlor. Barnaby had a few seconds of awkwardness, when his face stiffened and his shoulders stiffened and he couldn't meet Marcus's eyes, but Marcus greeted him with easy cheer and pulled out the chair alongside him.

Let it go, Barnaby told himself. Last night he had, without even meaning to. He and Marcus had worked alongside each other as if they were friends again, as if that afternoon with Lavinia had never happened.

He tried to relax his face, tried to relax his shoulders, but a kernel of awkwardness remained, sitting uncomfortably in his chest.

The servants brought more eggs, sirloin, and another teapot. "You planning on exploring that cavern?" Barnaby asked, in as neutral a tone as he could manage. "See where that other exit goes? Or will you seal the whole thing off?"

Marcus chewed, and thought. "I wouldn't mind exploring."

Their eyes met. Barnaby found himself grinning. "When?"

Marcus chewed another mouthful, considering this question. "Tomorrow. I'm going to be lazy today."

BARNABY DECIDED TO be lazy, too. At Lady Cosgrove's suggestion, they all strolled in the walled gardens. Espaliered fruit trees were trained along the south-facing walls, their branches thick with blossom.

"See that?" Miss Merryweather said, pointing at a small wooden block inset in the stone wall. "In winter they take out all those blocks and light fires inside the walls, to heat the gardens."

"They do?" Barnaby stepped closer. Yes, each block had a ring attached so it could be pulled out. "I've heard of such things."

"He'll want to see inside the wall now, Merry," Marcus said, and a quick glance showed that Marcus looked as amused as he sounded. "Barnaby likes to know how things work."

Miss Merryweather took him to view the hollow wall. "Fascinating," Barnaby said, and wished he could see the system in action.

Marcus and his wife had wandered to the far side of the garden, hand in hand. They looked as if they'd like to kiss. Miss Merryweather must have thought so too, for she glanced at them, and steered Barnaby along a path that led into one of the kitchen gardens.

"The gardeners plant flowers in with the vegetables," Miss Merryweather said. "See all the marigolds and nasturtiums? They help keep the insects away."

"They do?"

"One of the gardeners told me. Plants are quite interesting, you know."

Barnaby nodded, and found himself telling her about cocksfoot and lucerne, and how if you planted them, you could maintain *three* times as many sheep—

And then he realized what he was doing. He felt himself go red. "I beg your pardon, Miss Merryweather."

"Whatever for?"

"For prosing on about agriculture."

"Because, being a female, I can't possibly find it interesting?" She opened her eyes wide and fixed him with a stare.

Barnaby felt his face become even redder. That sharp, blue stare seemed to skewer him like a rapier. "Of course not."

Dimples peeked in Miss Merryweather's cheeks. To his relief, Barnaby realized she was roasting him. "Agriculture is a topic that bores most people, male or female," he said, more certain of his ground.

"And yet, we all rely upon it." Miss Merryweather took his arm, and led him down a path between beds of vegetables. "Marcus says you're better than any bailiff when it comes to land management."

Barnaby blinked. "He does?"

"He says that any tenant who has you for a landlord is extremely fortunate."

Barnaby felt himself blush again. "I would hope my decisions improve their livelihoods."

"Marcus says you like to understand things inside *and* out, and that the practice interests you even more than the theory. He said he's seen you plant crops and help with lambing and dig out ditches."

"I like to know how things are done," Barnaby said, uncomfortably. Had Marcus done nothing but talk about him?

"Marcus says—"

"Marcus says a great deal too much!"

Miss Merryweather glanced at him. Her dimples became very pronounced. She was silently laughing at him. "Do you wish to change the subject?"

"Yes," Barnaby said.

"What would you like to talk about?"

Barnaby stared down at Miss Merryweather, and wanted—quite shockingly—to kiss her. He wrenched his gaze from her face. "Tell me about the monks who built this place."

THEY SPENT AN hour in the gardens—during which time he and Miss Merryweather discussed Augustinian monks, balloon ascensions, Shakespeare, and the skill of Marcus's French chef. Miss Merryweather made him laugh three times, and each time she did, Barnaby wanted to kiss her. He took care to keep his distance from her, to look at her no more often than was polite, but it was difficult when her conversation was so invigorating and he enjoyed her company so much and she had such captivating dimples.

They all returned to the abbey, to discover that the chef had produced a tray of particularly French and particularly irresistible pastries. Miss Merryweather clapped her hands in delight. "Look at them!"

Barnaby was looking. Each dainty pastry was a masterpiece in itself. He saw tiny slices of glazed fruit, and whipped cream and powdered sugar, and three shades of chocolate. His mouth began to water.

"I'm going to have to increase Guillaume's wages again," Marcus said, eyeing the laden tray.

They settled in the drawing room, with the French doors open to the cloister and the scent of roses drifting in.

Barnaby watched Miss Merryweather examine the tray, watched her choose two pastries, watched her tease Marcus over his own selection.

The day they'd met, she'd said people called her Merry because it was less of a mouthful. She was wrong. They called her

Merry because she had the gift of laughter, and because Merry was the name that suited her above all others in the world.

I like her. In fact, he liked her too much. More than any other female he'd met. Not because she was pretty—although she was extremely pretty—but because of who she was: observant and shrewd and plainspoken and funny.

He studied her face for a moment, heart-shaped, with wide cheekbones and a delicately pointed chin. Such clear blue eyes. Such a full, sweet mouth. And behind those things, such a quick, keen mind.

Miss Merryweather said something that made Marcus and Lady Cosgrove both laugh. She grinned, dimples peeking in her cheeks, and Barnaby's heart seemed to lurch in his chest.

He looked abruptly down at his plate. *For God's sake, Bee, don't fall in love with her*. He was an adulterer. He would carry that label the rest of his life. And as an adulterer, he was no husband for a respectable young woman.

CHAPTER TEN

April 9th, 1807
Devonshire

MARCUS AND SIR Barnaby set off to explore the cave in the morning, with four of the outdoors servants. By noon, they still hadn't returned. Merry took to twisting her handkerchief. "Relax," Charlotte told her, feeding Charles in the sunlit nursery. "Marcus promised they'd take no risks."

"But what if the roof falls on their heads!"

"It won't. Sit down and stop shredding that poor handkerchief—and tell me, am I wrong in thinking that Sir Barnaby is . . ." Charlotte's brow creased as she searched for a word. "Easing?"

Merry sat, and allowed herself to be distracted. "You're not wrong. He's growing more comfortable with Marcus and he's a lot easier in himself."

"Good. That's what I thought—but I don't have your eyes."

Merry smoothed out her handkerchief, and folded it. "Sir Barnaby needs a little time to adjust his thinking. Remember how long it took Marcus? It didn't happen overnight."

Charlotte looked dismayed. "Are you saying it could be months?"

"No. I think he's almost there. The rescue in the caves helped a lot." Merry folded her handkerchief even smaller. "I think . . .

this is going to sound silly, but . . . after what happened with Lavinia, I think Sir Barnaby dug a pit for himself—a metaphorical pit—and he locked himself away at the bottom of it—and that day Marcus visited, he tried to climb up out of it, but Marcus kicked him back down, and this time, even though Marcus has handed him a rope and is trying to pull him up, he's not sure whether he should climb out or not. He thinks he *deserves* to stay at the bottom of his pit." She glanced up at Charlotte, and felt herself flush faintly. "Silly, I know."

Charlotte shook her head. "No, it makes sense. Marcus *did* kick him down. Metaphorically. I saw it." She adjusted Charles slightly. "I hope he does manage to climb out. Marcus needs this friendship. It's very important to him. His parents were . . ." She grimaced. "Marcus might have been the coal hauler's boy, for all the attention they paid him. Sir Barnaby wasn't just his best friend; he was his *family*."

Merry nodded soberly. Marcus rarely spoke of his parents.

Charlotte sighed, and gently stroked Charles's head. "Plus, most of Marcus's friendships are political. He needs someone he can relax with and talk about things *other* than politics."

"He does that with you."

"Well, yes, but I can't talk about guns and boxing and all those things men like to talk about. He tried to discuss the great pugilists with me once, when he thought I was a man, and soon gave up." She laughed, and shook her head. "Although, he did teach me how to box. That was fun."

Merry lifted her eyebrows. "Marcus taught you to box?"

"A little. He said I had a natural aptitude." Charlotte grinned. "I'll show you later, if you like."

AT TWO O'CLOCK, the men returned, filthy, disheveled, and bursting with excitement.

"You *have* to come see it," Marcus said. "It's incredible!"

"It goes on and *on*," Sir Barnaby said, his hazel eyes alight. "Passages and caverns. And look! Look what I found!" He dug in one pocket and fished out a small, flat, round object tarnished with verdigris.

"A coin?"

"Yes, but *look* at it!" Sir Barnaby held it out to her. "It's Roman!"

Merry took the object, and examined it. It was indeed a Roman coin, thin and not perfectly round, stamped with a head on one side and—she squinted—a ship on the other. *Perhaps I won't have to look far for my hoard of treasure?*

She passed the coin to Charlotte.

"You *have* to come see it," Marcus said again.

"Absolutely," Charlotte said, inspecting the coin. "When? Now?"

"Tomorrow," Marcus said. "The entrance needs a little work."

"Is it safe?" Merry asked dubiously.

"The main cavern is perfectly safe," Sir Barnaby assured her. "The smaller ones . . ." He exchanged a glance with Marcus, and shrugged. "They appear safe."

Merry pressed her lips together. All roofs appeared safe until they fell on one's head.

"Don't go any further than the main cavern, if you don't want to," Sir Barnaby said. "But you *have* to see that, Miss Merryweather. It's a wonderland!" He'd completely forgotten about his villainy. All his stiffness, his awkwardness, his inner misery, were gone. "Marcus found something, too. Show them, Marcus!"

Merry sat back and watched the two men, not fully listening to their words. There was ease in the way they spoke to each other, ease in the way they sat shoulder to shoulder, knees bumping, ease in the way Sir Barnaby reached across and turned whatever it was over on Marcus's palm. They were eager, enthusiastic, excited, shedding dirt and dust on the sofa, finishing each other's sentences. Merry eyed them thoughtfully. *This is what they were like when they were boys. As close as brothers.*

Sir Barnaby held whatever it was out to her. "Look!"

Merry took it—and blinked. "A tooth?" And not just any tooth. A carnivore's fang that was longer than her thumb, gray and pitted with age. She stared at Marcus, her mouth half-open in astonishment. "You found this?"

A grin split his dirty face.

Merry looked at the tooth, and at the Roman coin in Charlotte's hand, and suddenly *she* was bursting with excitement, too. "I want to see this cave."

MERRY WAS LESS certain of her decision the next afternoon, when she stood at the entrance to the cave wearing her oldest walking dress, her oldest shawl, her oldest gloves, and her sturdiest boots. The aperture was part crack in the hillside, and part excavation. The darkness inside seemed deep and dangerous. *Do I really want to do this?*

"You don't have to, Miss Merryweather, if you truly don't want to."

She glanced up and found Sir Barnaby watching her with an expression of such earnestness that she had to smile. "I do want to." And she *did*. She was just . . . a little nervous.

Marcus went first, then Charlotte, and then it was her turn. Merry took a deep breath and climbed into the hole, clutching her lantern tightly.

The passage was narrow and short, and she barely had time to become more nervous than she already was before it opened into a vast cavern.

Merry halted, staring.

"Incredible, isn't it?" Sir Barnaby said, coming to stand alongside her.

Merry nodded, speechless. He'd been correct yesterday: it *was* a wonderland.

The men had spent several hours here this morning. Now, she understood what they'd been doing. There were candles everywhere—on the floor, in niches, on ledges—casting golden light that turned the cavern into an enchanted palace. Pinnacles of rock thrust up from the floor and hung suspended from the ceiling, and on the far side of the chamber, she saw what looked like a waterfall of stone.

"The ones that hang down are called stalactites, and the ones that stand up are stalagmites," Sir Barnaby said quietly in her ear.

Merry nodded again, still speechless.

"Would you like to look around?"

Merry found her voice. "Yes."

Sir Barnaby gave her his arm, and Merry clutched it while they explored the cavern. The strange formations looked as if they were made of melting wax—and yet they were rock-hard to the touch. The waterfall was rock-hard, too. Even the thinnest and most fragile of the stalactites, looking like pieces of straw, were rock-hard.

At the back of her mind, Merry was aware of the weight of the hillside pressing down on her—rock, earth, trees—but the forefront of her mind was filled with wonder. She made a complete circuit of the cavern, and then went back to stare at the solidified rivulets that made up the stone waterfall.

"Impressive, isn't it?" Sir Barnaby said.

Merry nodded.

Footsteps crunched on the floor behind them. "I'm going to show Charlotte where we found the coin and the tooth," Marcus said. "Do you wish to come, Merry?"

Merry hesitated. She thought of the groom waiting outside with the horses and the picnic hamper—*I could sit in the sun and wait for them*—and then she fingered the pocket of her shawl, crammed with candles and a tinderbox. "I'll come."

Marcus led them along a large passageway. Candles flickered here, too. The air was cool and moist, smelling of damp earth. The passage twisted erratically. The roof grew lower. Another passage opened to the left, dark and unlit.

Merry's underlying nervousness blossomed into full-grown anxiety. Her awareness of the weight pressing down on them became stronger. Even the blackness that hovered beyond the candlelight seemed to have weight. She gripped Sir Barnaby's arm tightly. "How much further?"

"Another dozen yards or so." His hand covered hers on his arm. "Would you like to turn back?"

Merry shivered. *Yes.* "No," she said stoutly.

The passage ended in an array of caverns, small and large, opening out from one another like rooms in a house. Light flickered from half a hundred candles.

Marcus had found the tooth near a stalagmite shaped like a beehive. Encased in the rock at the base of the stalagmite were other toothlike lumps. "I think these are more of them," Marcus said, tracing the shapes with his fingers. "But there's no getting them out. Heaven only knows how long they've been here!"

"What animal do you think they're from?" Charlotte asked.

The men looked at each other and shrugged. "Bear?" Sir Barnaby said. "Wolf?"

"And the coin? Where did you find it?"

Sir Barnaby led them to one of the smaller chambers. On the far side was the entrance to yet another cave. The dark, gaping hole looked like a mouth. Merry repressed a shiver.

"It was lying here." Sir Barnaby stirred the dirt with the toe of his boot. "As if someone had dropped it."

It was very odd to think that a Roman had stood where they were standing now. Merry raised her lantern and gazed around. A rock seam snaked across the ceiling.

"What's in that cave?" Charlotte asked, pointing to the unlit mouth.

"We haven't had time to explore it yet. This place is an absolute warren."

"Is this cave safe?" Merry asked, her gaze on the snaking seam.

"It's been here for hundreds of years," Marcus said. "Maybe even thousands."

That doesn't mean the roof won't collapse, Merry thought—but didn't say aloud.

"To think that a *Roman* stood here . . ." Charlotte said, wonder in her voice. She crouched, placed her lantern on the floor, and began sifting through the dirt with her gloved hands.

They all searched for several minutes, and then the men started talking about teeth and claws and bones and skulls, and went back into the main cavern.

Charlotte stayed in the smaller chamber. "I should very much like to find a coin of my own," she confessed, and Merry recalled that Charlotte's father had been an antiquarian.

Merry glanced over her shoulder. Sir Barnaby and Marcus crouched beside the beehive stalagmite, heads bent close together. *Finding these caves was a blessing.* The men's friendship was whole again.

Charlotte climbed to her feet, picked up her lantern, and peered into the unlit cave.

Merry went to stand nervously alongside her. The cave was small and roughly circular, its floor several feet lower than where they now stood and its ceiling much higher. Straw-thin stalactites hung down. On the far side was the entrance to yet another cave, looking for all the world like a little arched door-way. *Gnomes live beyond there,* Merry thought.

"Look! Do you think those are coins?"

Merry looked where Charlotte was pointing. Several tiny, dark objects lay on the ground.

"They look as if they could be," Merry admitted "Shall I get Marcus?"

"No. These are *our* coins." Charlotte grinned at her, then crouched and jumped lightly down into the chamber.

Merry reluctantly followed. She raised her lantern and examined the roof. It *looked* safe, although there was another dark, twisting seam above her head.

"Coins," Charlotte said, with deep satisfaction in her voice.

"Roman?"

Charlotte held a coin close to the lantern and peered at it, her spectacles reflecting the light. "Yes." She stood, dusting her gown. "There are times I miss being a man, you know. Breeches are *so* much more practical than gowns."

"Charlotte! Merry!" a male voice bellowed.

"Down here," Charlotte called. "Don't panic. We found some more coins."

Merry doubted that Marcus heard her. The echoes of his shout boomed and reverberated, bouncing off the rock, so loud it seemed to shake the cave.

And then, with a gritty *whoomp,* part of the roof *did* collapse.

CHAPTER ELEVEN

DUST FILLED BARNABY'S eyes, filled his mouth and nose, and noise filled his ears—booms and cracks—rebounding and echoing until it sounded as if the entire cave system were collapsing around them.

Gradually the noise died to a clatter of rolling stones. Barnaby found himself on hands and knees, blind, half-deaf. Each inhalation brought more dust, choking him.

He coughed, blinked, and lurched to his feet. No, not blind. He saw candlelight, and air thick with dust, and another lurching shape: Marcus.

Barnaby blinked again. Before, he'd been standing in the entrance to the cave where he'd found the coin, empty of Lady Cosgrove and Miss Merryweather, with a dark opening gaping on the far side; now, he was standing in the entrance to . . . disaster. Half the cave's roof had come down, and the dark opening was gone.

"Christ." Horror held him frozen for a moment—and then panic took over. He began frantically heaving chunks of limestone aside. "Miss Merryweather! Lady Cosgrove!" Dust rose from the rubble, as if the rocks were smoking.

Marcus joined him, flinging rocks aside. They worked silently, frantically.

A sound caught Barnaby's attention. He grabbed Marcus's

arm. "Listen."

Marcus froze, his head up, questing.

The sound came again, faint and far away. "Marcus?"

"Charlotte?" Marcus bellowed. He began scrambling up the pile of rubble. Another chunk of rock detached itself from the ceiling, almost hitting him.

Barnaby caught Marcus's arm and hauled him back. "Quiet!" he choked out. "If you shout, you'll bring it down on our heads."

He saw the struggle on Marcus's face—panic versus self-control. Self-control won. Marcus inhaled a shuddering breath. He turned back to the rubble. He didn't shake Barnaby's hand from his arm. "Charlotte?" His voice was pitched low, as quiet as if they were in church. "Can you hear me?"

"Yes," came the faint answer.

Barnaby tilted his head, trying to catch where her voice was coming from.

"Are you and Merry all right?" Marcus asked in the same, low voice.

"We're fine. Just a little . . . alarmed."

High up to the right, a hole gaped between the ceiling and the rockfall. Barnaby released Marcus's arm and pointed. "Up there." Dust caught in his throat and made him cough. "Her voice is coming from there."

Marcus nodded. He examined the rubble, examined the ceiling. "I'm going up."

"No, *I'm* going up. You get back out there." Barnaby jerked his thumb at the larger cavern behind them.

Breath hissed between Marcus's teeth. "She's *my* wife—"

"You have a son, Marcus! If the rest of the roof comes down, one of you needs to survive, else Charles will grow up an orphan."

When Marcus was angry, his face became bony. It became bony now. Very bony. "Damn you for being right!" He swung away and strode out to the larger cavern, hands clenched.

Barnaby turned back to the rockfall. "Lady Cosgrove? Miss Merryweather? Stand as far back as you can. I'm going to see if that hole's big enough to get you out."

He waited several seconds, then began to climb the rubble. Chunks of rock rolled and shifted beneath his boots, rattling to the ground. When he was nearly at the top, he dislodged a huge slab. It slid down the pile like a toboggan, slamming heavily into the cave floor, sending echoes reverberating.

Barnaby continued warily, creeping on hands and knees, on his belly, his head almost brushing the crumbling roof. The hole was about a foot and a half high and nearly three feet wide. He wriggled carefully forward, and peered into the cave beyond.

Half the ceiling had detached in one large chunk that sloped steeply away from him to bury itself in the chamber floor. It looked like a giant's tombstone. Beyond it, on the farthest side of the chamber, stood Miss Merryweather and Lady Cosgrove.

His gaze skipped over Lady Cosgrove, and settled on Miss Merryweather. She stood gripping her cousin's hand. His eyes made the same mistake they'd made the very first time he'd seen her, telling him she was a child. A small, dusty, waiflike child. And then he blinked, and saw her for who she truly was. Small and dusty, yes, but not waiflike. Strong. Self-possessed. Resolute. Her posture was ramrod straight, her chin slightly up, as if defying anyone to call her scared.

Barnaby released the breath he'd been holding. *She's unhurt.* "Are you all right?" he asked, quietly.

"Perfectly," Lady Cosgrove said, her voice cool and calm.

Barnaby tore his gaze from Miss Merryweather and examined the slab of rock. He touched it cautiously, and then less cautiously, and then pressed as hard as he could. It didn't shift so much as an inch. To his eyes it seemed safer than the sliding pile of rubble on his side—but its sheerness made it impossible for the women to climb, and the floor of the chamber was a good fifteen feet below the hole. "We need some kind of ladder to get you out. It'll take us a while to fetch it. Um . . . try not to make any noise."

"There's a small grotto behind this cave," Lady Cosgrove said. "It looks quite safe. We'll wait there."

"Do you have spare candles?" Both ladies, he was pleased to see, still had their lanterns.

"I brought six candles and a tinderbox," Miss Merryweather said, and then she smiled wryly. "Just in case."

Courage and common sense, *and* a sense of humor. Barnaby felt his heart give a little stutter. *I think I love you, Miss Merryweather.* He cleared his throat. "I'll fetch some blankets. Try not to worry too much. We'll get you out."

HE CLIMBED BACK down the rockfall and went out into the cavern where they'd found the tooth. Marcus pounced on him. "Well?"

Barnaby described the second chamber. "We'll need a rope ladder to get them out."

"I'll fetch one." Marcus spun on his heel.

"And send the groom in with those blankets for the picnic. And the candles we had left over. We need more light—and so do they."

"Will do." Marcus ran from the cavern. Barnaby heard the *tap-tap-tap* of his boots and then that sound faded. He went back into the smaller chamber and stared at the pile of rubble.

Fifteen minutes later, the groom arrived, a bulky picnic hamper in his arms, two blankets over one shoulder, and a rope wound around his waist.

Barnaby hastily relieved him of the hamper. "Thank you, Sawyer," he whispered. "Keep your voice down."

The groom glanced warily into the small chamber. "His lord-ship said to give the hamper to the ladies, if we can."

"We'll try. The candles?"

Sawyer dug into his pockets and produced four candles. "I put the rest of 'em in the hamper."

Barnaby placed the hamper on the floor and opened it. It had been hurriedly repacked. "I left in the food," Sawyer whispered. "But I took out most of the glasses and plates, so's I could fit in all the lemonade. Thought they'd need something to drink."

"Good thinking."

Barnaby lit the four extra candles and placed them around the small chamber. Then he and Sawyer climbed the rockfall, lug-ging the hamper and the blankets. There wasn't enough space for them both at the top. Sawyer, the ex-pugilist, was a hulking man; it was easy to imagine him jamming fast in the hole. "Stay here," Barnaby breathed. "Pass the stuff to me."

He inched forward on his belly and stared into the next cave. The huge slab hadn't moved. It still looked like a giant's grave-stone, its foot buried in the cave floor, its head resting just below his chin. Opposite him, low in the cave wall, was a hole shaped like a small doorway; the entrance to the grotto Lady Cosgrove had spoken of.

The blankets unrolled as they slid down the slab, arriving at the bottom with a faint, sighing *swooop*. The hamper was more difficult; it took their combined efforts to shove it through the gap. Several chunks of rock dislodged, rattling to the floor.

Barnaby lowered the hamper on the end of the rope. The grit-ty, sliding sound it made brought both ladies from the grotto. He beckoned them forward.

They untied the hamper, gathered up the blankets, and re-treated to the far side of the chamber, where they stood, looking up at him.

Barnaby stared down at Miss Merryweather, at her dusty, disheveled ringlets and pale, heart-shaped face and determined composure. "Shouldn't be more than an hour or two," he said, in a low voice.

Both ladies nodded.

Barnaby hesitated. Should he try to haul them up now, using the rope? Between him and Sawyer, they ought to be strong enough. But it would be like a wrestling match at the top, and the gap wasn't big enough for him *and* someone else, and more rock *would* come down.

No, it was safer to wait for a ladder.

Barnaby coiled up the rope. "We'll get you out. I give you my word."

BY THE TIME Marcus returned, Barnaby and Sawyer had enlarged the gap as much as they dared. With every movement they made, rubble shifted beneath them. Twice, large chunks tobogganed to the floor, striking with great cracks of sound. The second time this happened, a shower of stones fell from the ceiling, making them both duck. The clatter from that was just dying—and Barnaby's heartbeat returning to something approaching normal—when Marcus arrived. He brought three gardeners and two stablemen with him, and shovels, ropes, and a rope ladder that had been hastily cobbled together.

Barnaby and Sawyer scrambled down to meet them.

"How are they?" Marcus asked, his eyes fierce with anxiety.

"In good spirits. That roof's damned fragile, though."

They attached a rope to one end of the ladder and looped it around a stalagmite. "I'll go through and help them climb," Barnaby said. "We need a man at the top, to help them, and one about halfway down. Not your biggest men; the ones who can move the most stealthily."

Marcus ran his eye over the assembled men, and selected a

gardener and one of the grooms. "Noake . . . and Rudkin." Both men were young and wiry.

"Everyone else needs to stay well back."

Marcus nodded.

Barnaby turned to Sawyer. "Sawyer, if that roof *does* come down, get him out of here—even if you have to put him in a headlock to do it—and don't let him back in."

"Yes, sir."

"Damn it, Bee—"

"Think about Charles."

"I *am* thinking about Charles," Marcus snarled. "Or it would be *me* climbing through, not you!"

Barnaby met his eyes, and nodded. He picked up the rope ladder and turned away. Marcus followed. "For God's sake, Bee, be careful."

"I will."

Marcus caught his arm, and said in a whisper, "Tell Charlotte to use her gift if she thinks it will help."

"What?"

"She'll understand." Marcus released his arm. "Be careful."

BARNABY CLIMBED THE rockfall for the third time that after-noon, the anchor rope trailing behind him. He stationed the stableman halfway up, and the gardener at the top, then crept through the gap. Nothing had changed on the other side.

He released the rope ladder. It unrolled with a gritty slither-ing sound, the bottom two rungs slapping on the ground.

"Tell them to tie off the rope," he whispered to the gardener.

The anchor rope pulled taut.

Barnaby began his descent. When he reached the third rung, the great slab shifted, settling several inches with a grating noise.

He froze, clinging to the ladder, his heart beating triple time in his chest.

The echoes died into silence. Barnaby released his breath in a slow trickle, and descended another rung. The giant's grave-stone dropped two feet with a sudden, jolting jerk. He lost his grip and slid down the slab amid an avalanche of stones, hit the floor hard enough to knock the breath from his lungs, and curled himself in a helpless ball. Stones thudded into him like dozens of bony fists.

When the clatter of falling rocks had faded, Barnaby uncurled fractionally. *God, I hope Noake and Rudkin are all right.*

He rolled over on his back, blinked gritty eyes, and gazed up at the gap. It had shrunk to the size of a rabbit hole.

"Sir Barnaby!" Someone leaned over him. "Sir Barnaby! Are you all right?"

Barnaby blinked, and focused on Miss Merryweather's face. Anxiety shone in her eyes as brightly as tears.

He reached out to lay his hand on her cheek, remembered himself in time, and changed the movement into a general un-curling of his body. "I'm fine." He pushed up to sit, and coughed twice. "I'm fine," he repeated. "But we have a slight problem."

CHAPTER TWELVE

SIR BARNABY CLIMBED to his feet with the slow caution of a man who was almost certain he had no broken bones. He was as filthy as a chimney sweep. Relief at seeing him stand made the urge to cry even stronger. Merry blinked back her tears with determination. She was *not* going to cry.

"Bee! Barn-a-*bee!*" a faint, frantic voice called.

Sir Barnaby turned towards the rockfall. "I'm fine," he called back, his voice low. "Are Noake and Rudkin all right?"

"Not hurt."

"Thank God," Sir Barnaby said, and then he pitched his voice to carry: "Sawyer, get his lordship out of there. Now."

"I'm trying, sir."

"Well, try harder," Sir Barnaby muttered. He raked a hand through his hair, dislodging dust and grit, and turned to face her and Charlotte. "We'll get out of here," he said, with utter confidence. "It'll just take a little longer, is all. Now, let's get into that grotto. This cave's not safe."

"Sir Barnaby?" a low voice called. Not Marcus.

They all turned back to the rockfall. "Yes?"

"We're going to clear as much of this rubble as we can and shore the roof with timber. Could take all night."

"For heaven's sake, don't rush," Sir Barnaby said. "Take it slowly. Doesn't matter how long it takes, just as long as no one's hurt."

"Yes, sir."

"God, I hope they're careful," he said, under his breath, and then he turned back to her and Charlotte, and smiled cheerfully. "Show me this grotto, ladies."

SIR BARNABY GAVE a low whistle. "This looks like something out of a storybook."

"Yes," Merry said, clutching her hands together, and trying to sound calm.

The grotto was the size of her bedroom in Woodhuish Abbey. Its ceiling was a dozen feet at the highest point, but less than three feet in the lowest corner. In half a dozen places, stalactites and stalagmites had joined to form slender, graceful columns.

"It makes me think of *A Midsummer Night's Dream,*" Charlotte said. "I can imagine Titania here."

Sir Barnaby crossed to the nearest column and patted it. "This'll keep the roof up."

"Yes," Merry said again. *Don't panic, don't panic.* But she was aware of the weight of rock and earth above her, crushingly heavy. She forced herself to smile, and peeled her hands apart. "There are three more caves off this one. One has bones in it, and the strangest skull, and teeth like the one Marcus found."

Sir Barnaby's head jerked around. "What?"

"The bones are as hard as rock," Charlotte said. "They're stuck to the floor."

"This, I *have* to see."

SIR BARNABY WAS delighted with the bones. "This is incredible! I don't suppose either of you has a sketch pad?" He crouched and fingered the skull. "My God, what a gift to find something like this!" And then he paused, and frowned, and looked up at Charlotte. "Marcus said . . . Marcus told me to tell you to use your gift, if it would help. He said you'd understand what he meant."

Merry understood what it meant, too. She exchanged a glance with Charlotte.

"There might be a sketch pad in the hamper," Charlotte said. "I'll look."

Merry gave Sir Barnaby a bright smile, and followed Charlotte. "You should go," she whispered, once they were back in the grotto.

"I can't leave you here!" Charlotte whispered back.

"Yes, you can. Sir Barnaby's here. I won't be alone."

Charlotte's expression was miserable and indecisive.

"*Go,* Charlotte. It's stupid staying, if you can get out. Think about Charles!"

Charlotte hugged her breasts as if they hurt. "I need to feed him . . ."

"Then *go.*" Merry pushed Charlotte towards the little arch-shaped exit. They both peered out at the rockfall. "Can you get through that hole?"

"Yes," Charlotte said, and then: "But Merry, I *can't*. I have to keep my magic secret. If it becomes common knowledge . . ." She hugged herself more tightly. "It scares people. Marcus almost shot me, the first time he saw me do it."

Merry nibbled on her lip. "Only show yourself to the nursemaid," she suggested. "And Marcus, of course. Let everyone else think you're here. Brough's a sensible woman. She'll keep your secret. Once the rockfall is cleared, come back and be seen to leave with us."

Charlotte looked dubious. "You think it will serve?"

"Yes," Merry said firmly. *The fewer of us stuck down here, the fewer of us who can die.* "Tell Brough the truth: that you have a Faerie godmother. She's too level-headed to fly into hysterics. And she loves Charles. She'll keep the secret for your sake *and* his sake."

"And Sir Barnaby? He'll have to know, too."

"Sir Barnaby will be fascinated. You're much more remarkable than an old skeleton."

Charlotte huffed a wry laugh. "Thank you. I think."

"Lady Cosgrove? Miss Merryweather? Is everything all right?"

Sir Barnaby stood behind them, his face filthy and alert.

Charlotte took a deep breath. "Sir Barnaby, there's something I must tell you."

SIR BARNABY DIDN'T believe the tale about the Faerie godmother. Merry saw it on his face; beneath the careful politeness was a flicker of alarm. *He thinks Charlotte's gone mad.*

But he *did* believe when Charlotte removed her shawl and her spectacles, and knelt on the floor and changed into a monkey.

His mouth gaped open and he stared with such stunned incredulity that Merry almost laughed. He watched, speechless, as the monkey climbed out the neckhole of Charlotte's gown, changed into a sparrow, and flitted up to perch on Merry's shoulder. The sparrow gave a chirp—Goodbye? Be careful?—and flew out of the grotto.

They both hurried to peer into the debris-strewn cave beyond.

Charlotte was already gone.

"Good Lord," Sir Barnaby said in a faint, awed voice, and then he turned to Merry. "What on earth?"

"YOU HAVE A Faerie godmother, too?" Sir Barnaby said, when she'd finished explaining.

Merry nodded. "And I'll receive my gift on my twenty-fifth birthday. The day after tomorrow."

"Good Lord," Sir Barnaby said again. He blinked several times. "Will Charles . . . ?"

"No. Only the women in our line."

His gaze was intent, fascinated. "What will you choose?"

Merry hugged her knees. "I don't know. I've had years to think about it, and I'm still not sure. Charlotte only found out on her twenty-fifth birthday, and she had minutes to decide, and she made the perfect choice for her. She wanted to earn her living, so she chose metamorphosis and became a man. She was Marcus's secretary, you know."

Sir Barnaby's dusty eyebrows climbed higher. "His secretary?"

Merry nodded. "You saw him once. Or rather, her."

"I did?"

"She was with Marcus when he visited you at Mead Hall."

Sir Barnaby's face tightened, as if her words had been a slap. She saw emotions chase themselves across his face—dismay, mortification—before his expression congealed into masklike blankness.

Idiot. You shouldn't have told him Charlotte witnessed that meeting.

"If we're still here on my birthday, I'll use my gift to get us out," Merry said hastily, to distract him. "I can do that, you know: choose a one-off gift, rather than a permanent one. Although most of the one-offs tend to be healing of some kind or other. One of my ancestresses was wall-eyed, and she used her gift to fix that." She was gabbling, the words spilling over one another. "But I hope we're out of here before then, because I *would* like a gift that lasts my life. Although . . . being alive would last my life, I guess."

Sir Barnaby gave her a polite, unfelt smile. His attention was directed inwards.

Merry plowed on. "There are dozens of different gifts, you know. Some of them have warnings, because they can drive you mad, or . . . or make things worse than they already are. Like resurrection. You mustn't *ever* resurrect a dead person. Someone tried that, back in the sixteenth century—her husband had died—and his body became alive again, but he was a raving lunatic."

Sir Barnaby blinked. She'd caught his attention.

"I thought I might choose finding things as my gift," Merry confessed. "So I can find a hoard of treasure, and not need to rely on Charlotte and Marcus's charity. But it seems very selfish, and I can't help thinking that I should choose a gift that helps people. Although, if I chose finding things I could find lost children, like Clem and Harry, and *that* wouldn't be selfish." She paused, her eyes on his face. *Say something, Sir Barnaby.*

After a few seconds, he did. "Marcus and Charlotte clearly enjoy having you in their household. Your keep would be inconsequential to them."

"To them, yes. To me, no." Merry looked at the hem of her gown and brushed at the dirt there, then looked back at him. "My father did leave me an inheritance, but it's not enough to last my lifetime, and the only career I'm fitted for is dancing, and I will *not* be an opera dancer."

Sir Barnaby rocked back slightly. "I should hope not."

"And I can't be a dancing master because I'm a female." Merry sighed. "It would be so much easier if I were a man."

Sir Barnaby blinked. The closed-in expression had gone from his face. He looked bemused.

Successfully distracted. Merry smiled cheerfully at him. "Would you like some food?"

Sir Barnaby blinked again. "I suppose we had better eat."

"There's water seeping down the wall, just past that skeleton.

Enough to dampen a handkerchief with. Charlotte and I used it to wash our faces."

"Ah." Sir Barnaby's eyes lit up. He climbed to his feet.

CHAPTER THIRTEEN

THEY ATE AND drank sparingly from the hamper; Sir Barnaby was of the opinion that it would be morning before sufficient rubble had been cleared and the roof shored up with timber. He quenched all the candles, including the one in Charlotte's lantern. The only light came from her own lantern—one single, flickering, golden flame. The grotto became dark and shadowy, but instead of being frightening, it was strangely cozy. Her awareness of the weight pressing down on them had faded. What she was mostly aware of, was Sir Barnaby. They sat with their backs to a wall, side by side, wrapped in blankets. Their shoulders touched—the lightest of pressures, barely felt—and yet Merry was vividly conscious of it, vividly conscious of Sir Barnaby's quiet breathing, of his presence alongside her.

The disconcerting shyness that had stricken her at the ball returned. She felt self-conscious and bashful and inarticulate.

Why am I so shy?

Because she was head over heels in love with Sir Barnaby. Because she desperately wanted him to love her back. Because she didn't know whether he did.

He liked her—of that, she was certain—but he didn't look at her with his heart in his eyes, the way Marcus looked at Charlotte. He was courteous and friendly and cheerful and, most of all, kind. His shoulder was touching hers because he knew she was afraid, because he was letting her know she wasn't alone, because he was trying to make her feel safe.

And it was working. She did feel safe. She sat in the almost-dark, with the weight of a hillside resting on top of them, and *knew* she should be scared, but she wasn't.

Because Sir Barnaby was with her.

AN HOUR LATER, the grotto felt much less cozy. Cold seeped from the rock floor, from the walls. Merry hunched into the blanket and shivered. "Cold?" Sir Barnaby asked.

"Freezing," she admitted.

"Um . . ." Sir Barnaby said. "We'd conserve warmth if we, um . . . Do you mind if we touch?"

Merry's awareness of him flared—and with it, the shyness. "No."

Sir Barnaby cautiously put an arm around her.

"That doesn't help much," Merry confessed several minutes later, still shivering.

"No, it doesn't, does it?" Sir Barnaby hesitated, and then said, "Pretend I'm your father," and he picked her up, blanket and all, and settled her on his lap as if she were a child, tucking her inside his own blanket, putting his arms around her.

Merry stiffened—not in offense, but in a surfeit of shyness—and then forced herself to relax. "That's much better. Thank you." She rested her head against his chest and closed her eyes. Sir Barnaby smelled strongly of rock dust, and beneath that, of sweat and horse and sandalwood soap.

She thought of Henry. Stocky, dark-haired Henry, with his bulldog face and blunt way of speaking. Henry, whom she'd loved. Whom she always would love.

Henry, dead at sea four years ago.

Merry inhaled Sir Barnaby's dust-sweat-horse-soap smell

again, drawing it into her lungs, and felt a deep ache of love. Love for Henry. Love for Sir Barnaby.

On the surface, Sir Barnaby was nothing like Henry, but underneath, he was very similar. He had the same practical nature, the same vigorous, inquiring mind, the same kindness.

You would have liked Henry, if you had known him, she told Sir Barnaby silently, and she breathed in his scent again, and felt the ache, and the certainty. Certainty to the very marrow of her bones.

This man.

MERRY HAD NO idea how many hours she slept, but when she woke, she was shivering again. The grotto was pitch black; the lantern had gone out—but with Sir Barnaby's arms around her, she didn't feel afraid. "Are you awake?" she whispered.

"Yes."

"Are you cold?"

She felt him shiver. "Yes."

"We need to move." She uncurled stiffly and clambered off his lap. "Where's that tinderbox?"

"Here." Sir Barnaby lit another candle and placed it in the lantern. Light flickered across his weary face. His hair looked like a hayrick.

"Let's dance."

Astonishment crossed his face. "Here?"

"Of course, here. There's room enough, if we're careful."

Sir Barnaby glanced at the highest point of the grotto roof. "I suppose there is." He climbed to his feet, moving slowly. "Lord, I feel like an old man."

He looked rather like one at this moment, his hair gray with dust. Merry wanted to hug him; instead, she busied herself with the hamper. "Here, have some lemonade. And would you like some of these grapes? They're from Marcus's estate in Kent."

The sweet, juicy grapes and tart, thirst-quenching lemonade cleared the cavern taste from Merry's mouth. Sir Barnaby looked rather more alert. "All right," she said briskly. "Let's start with a minuet."

They took their places opposite one another. Shyness ambushed her again. She felt suddenly as gauche and awkward as a schoolroom chit. Merry took a deep breath. *Don't be silly,* she told herself. *You're twenty-five, not fifteen.*

Sir Barnaby bowed, Merry curtsied.

Sir Barnaby had taken off his gloves to eat. So had Merry. When their bare fingers touched, her awareness of him intensified sharply. Her heart gave a little kick in her chest, and began to beat faster.

Sir Barnaby held her fingertips lightly, and yet Merry's whole hand burned. The heat spread as they danced, far more heat than the stately steps of the minuet deserved. Merry didn't feel cold or scared; she felt vividly alive, the blood humming in her veins.

"How about a reel?" Sir Barnaby suggested next.

They danced a reel, at the end of which they were laughing and capering like children.

"Whew!" Sir Barnaby said, panting. "Now I'm warm."

Merry laughed up at him and hugged her joy to herself. *This man.*

They gulped more lemonade, and then Merry said, "Would you like to learn a new dance? It's very fashionable in Vienna."

"Absolutely."

"It's called the waltz. It's quite simple. Triple time. The basic step is this." She demonstrated the man's step, counting *one,* two, three, *one,* two, three—and Sir Barnaby copied her. "Now, stand facing me, and take my right hand in your left, and your right hand goes at my waist, here, and I put my hand on your shoulder like this."

Their bare palms pressed together. Merry's shyness swept back. She found herself not quite able to meet Sir Barnaby's eyes. Her stomach tightened and her heartbeat began to hammer in her ears. "It can be as energetic as you like, but let's start at walking pace. *One,* two, three . . ."

Sir Barnaby picked the dance up in less than a minute. "Excellent," Merry said, trying to smother her shyness. "Now, add some turns if you can."

Sir Barnaby could.

"Excellent," Merry said again. "Let's go faster."

Faster, they went, up and down the grotto, and the faster they danced, the closer Sir Barnaby had to hold her. Indecent, critics had labeled the waltz, and Merry could see why. It was an intimate dance. Thrillingly intimate. Her shyness warred with a heady exhilaration.

When they were both short of breath, Merry called a halt. They stood for a moment, holding on to one another, panting.

Merry's heart began to thud even faster. *This man.*

She experienced an almost overwhelming impulse to stand on tiptoe and press her lips to his.

Sir Barnaby's gaze dropped to her mouth. He hastily released her and stepped back. "More lemonade, Miss Merryweather?" His voice was cool and polite, putting distance between them.

Merry hugged her arms. Had he felt the same impulse? "How much is left?"

Sir Barnaby turned to the hamper. "One and a half flasks."

"A little, then, please." A feeling of euphoria built in her chest. *I think he wants to kiss me.*

Sir Barnaby poured them both lemonade. Once he'd drained his glass, he glanced around and his expression became faintly embarrassed. "Perhaps we should, er, allocate a privy."

"There are three caves off this grotto. One has that skeleton, but the other two are empty. Charlotte and I thought we'd use them. One each."

His expression lightened. "Ah, good."

THEY USED THEIR respective privies, washed their hands in the water seeping down the passage wall, and then ate some ham and grapes from the hamper. Sir Barnaby was friendly, cheerful, courteous—and looked at her as little as he could. He offered her more grapes, refilled her glass, told her a string of anecdotes that made her laugh, and avoided meeting her eyes whenever possible.

Why?

Merry nibbled her grapes and observed him, and came to a conclusion: Sir Barnaby was attracted to her—but because he was a gentleman and they were trapped here together, he was trying very hard not to show it.

Sir Barnaby packed up the hamper, brought out his pocket watch, announced it was half past three, and suggested they try to sleep again. He shook out the blankets and handed her one, but this time, when they sat, his shoulder didn't quite touch hers.

Without that contact, Merry found herself acutely aware of the weight of earth and rock pressing down on them. She shuffled sideways until their shoulders touched. Sir Barnaby seemed to tense slightly. "You all right?" he said.

"A little scared," Merry admitted.

"We're going to get out of here," Sir Barnaby said firmly. "I promise you."

You can't promise that, Merry thought, but she said, "I know," as if she believed him.

They huddled in their blankets, side by side. The cold seeped through her blanket, seeped through her clothes, and the colder she became, the more she felt the weight of rock above them.

Thousands of tons of rock, poised to fall on them.

Merry tried to repress her fear and failed, tried to repress her shivers and failed.

"Cold?" Sir Barnaby asked.

Scared. "Yes."

He hesitated. "Would you like me to hold you again?"

"Yes, please," Merry whispered.

Sir Barnaby settled her on his lap and wrapped his blanket around her. For some reason, it made her want to cry. Her throat closed and her nose stung and her eyes burned, and it took all her self-control not to burst into tears.

Merry leaned her head against his chest and struggled to control her breathing. *Don't cry.* But it was almost impossible not to when Sir Barnaby held her like this, his arms around her, and when she knew that the slender columns holding the roof up were going to snap like twigs and the hillside was going to fall on them.

All of a sudden, Merry knew that she had to tell Sir Barnaby how she felt about him. She knew it with the same certainty that she knew the roof was going to fall. She *had* to tell him she loved him, because if she died without telling him, and he died without knowing, it would be the most terrible thing in the world.

She drew in a breath—and found her tongue paralyzed by more than shyness. Fear, that's what this sensation was: fear. Fear that Sir Barnaby would reject her.

Am I such a coward?

Father had always said that the hardest thing he'd ever done in his life was to ask a viscount's daughter to marry him—but he *had* had the courage to ask, and her mother the courage to accept, and it hadn't mattered at all that her mother had been disinherited because they'd been happy, truly happy.

Father had the courage to do this; therefore, so do I.

Merry took a deep breath. "Sir Barnaby, will you please marry me?"

CHAPTER FOURTEEN

SIR BARNABY STIFFENED. His arms withdrew from around her. "If you feel that I have compromised you, Miss Merryweather, of course I will marry you," he said woodenly.

Merry scrambled off his lap. "What? Of course I don't think that! I'm asking you because I *want* to marry you!"

Sir Barnaby physically flinched. "Miss Merryweather, I'm not a good choice of husband."

"Stuff and nonsense!" Merry said. "If you don't wish to marry me, that's fine, but you can't use *that* as a reason."

Sir Barnaby's mouth tightened. "I'm an adulterer," he said flatly. "I'm the last person you should marry."

Merry stared at him, and made a discovery. Sir Barnaby had rebuilt his friendship with Marcus, but he hadn't forgiven himself. "Do you believe you'll commit adultery again?"

Sir Barnaby's expression became affronted, as if she had offered him a profound insult. "Of course not!"

"Then I fail to see the relevance of your objection."

"I'm not a fit husband for any respectable woman!" Sir Barnaby wasn't wooden anymore; he was angry. "My reputation—"

"Is irrelevant. My father was a dancing master. In the eyes of polite society, it's *I* who am not respectable, not you."

Sir Barnaby frowned, and drew breath to argue.

"If you don't wish to marry me because I'm too old, or too

odd, or because of my breeding, then say so. But don't use your reputation as an excuse."

"It's not an excuse," Sir Barnaby said stiffly. "And you're not old or odd, and your breeding is perfectly respectable. Any man would be lucky to have you as a wife."

"Then will you marry me? Please?"

Sir Barnaby turned his head from her. "You deserve better."

Merry sat back on her heels. How to reach him? "You've punished yourself enough."

Sir Barnaby glanced at her, a frown biting between his eyebrows.

Merry leaned forward and said fiercely, "Come out of your dungeon, Sir Barnaby!"

He blinked. His eyebrows twitched up. "You *are* a little unusual."

Merry found herself smiling crookedly at him. She held out her hand. "Marry me? Please?"

Sir Barnaby hesitated, and then took her hand. She felt the warm strength of his fingers. His expression was a study in doubt. "Miss Merryweather . . ."

"When Henry died, I never thought I'd meet another man I'd want to marry. But I have. I've met you. And I *know* we'll be happy together. We *suit* each other."

Sir Barnaby didn't look convinced. His face was filled with misgiving and uncertainty. "Miss Merryweather, things will look different once we're out of here—"

"I've known for two days that I want to marry you," Merry told him. She leaned closer and kissed him.

Sir Barnaby tensed, almost a flinch.

Merry kissed him a second time—a gentle kiss that told him that she loved him, that she trusted him. *This is how it's meant to be. See?* A third gentle kiss, a fourth, inviting him to kiss her back.

For a long, agonizing moment Sir Barnaby held himself rigid—and then he relented. His kiss was hesitant.

Merry gave an inward sigh of relief. He was unlocking the door to his dungeon.

She shyly explored his lips, learning their shape, their texture, their taste. Sir Barnaby wasn't completely relaxed. He was still holding back, permitting the kiss but not committing wholeheartedly to it. One foot in his dungeon, one out.

Merry nipped his lower lip gently. *Open for me, please.*

After another hesitation, Sir Barnaby did.

Their tongues touched. Merry felt Sir Barnaby tremble. He groaned, low in his throat, and then his arms came strongly around her.

The kiss changed its tempo. Now that Sir Barnaby had broken free of his dungeon, he wasn't hesitant at all. Long, delicious, candlelit minutes passed. Somehow—and Merry didn't quite notice how—she ended up on Sir Barnaby's lap, and her arms were around his neck, and she was holding him quite as tightly as he was holding her, and they were kissing each other as if their lives depended on it. She felt dizzy, breathless, feverish, and quite exhilaratingly alive. She'd never felt quite this alive before, not even when she'd kissed Henry. But she and Henry had only kissed once like this. And then, he'd died.

A dreadful shiver of prescience crawled up Merry's spine and she *knew*—knew with utter certainty—that Sir Barnaby was going to die, too. Knew that they both were. Knew that the roof was going to fall on them, crush them, bury them.

The heat that had built in her evaporated as abruptly as a candle being snuffed. Her skin prickled in a shiver.

Sir Barnaby broke their kiss. "Cold?"

Scared. Merry tightened her arms around his neck. "I love you," she whispered against his throat.

"I love you, too. You are the most exceptional woman I've

ever met. There is no one in the world like you. No one." Sir Barnaby laid a light kiss on her hair. "Are you tired? Would you like to sleep?"

Sleep? No, she wanted to cram as much as she could into what little time they had. She wouldn't make the same mistake she'd made with Henry. She would kiss Sir Barnaby while she could, talk with him while she could, touch him, tell him she loved him. "No." Merry pressed her lips to Sir Barnaby's throat, to his jaw, to his mouth again.

The kiss made a swift crescendo from *dolce* to *furioso,* but it was fear that drove her this time, not passion. Fear of running out of time. Fear of losing Sir Barnaby. Fear of dying.

Sir Barnaby pulled back, panting. "Miss Merryweather, we really must—"

"Merry. Or Anne, if you prefer."

"Merry, we really must stop."

"No," Merry said seriously. "We really mustn't." Sir Barnaby looked half-wild. His filthy hair stood on end, his breathing was ragged, his cheeks hectically flushed. His pupils were fully dilated, his eyes so fiercely bright that they seemed to burn. *My kisses make him feel alive,* she realized, and that made her want to cry.

Merry laid her hand on his cheek, feeling the heat of his skin and the faint prickle of his stubble. "Barnaby . . . will you please make love to me?"

CHAPTER FIFTEEN

BARNABY STIFFENED IN shock. "What?"

"Please?"

Barnaby took Merry's hand from his cheek, and held it in both of his. "No," he told her gently. "Of course not. We'll wait till we're married."

"We might never get a chance to be married!" Tears brimmed in her eyes. "This may be all the time we have."

She's right, a voice said in Barnaby's head. He ignored it. "Merry, I'm filthy, and there's no bed, and you're frightened. That's not how it should be."

"Henry and I were never intimate, and that's what I regret the most—because he's *dead*—" The tears spilled down her cheeks. "What if we're dead tomorrow? What then?"

Then I shall regret refusing you.

Barnaby released her hand and carefully wiped away her tears. Her skin was soft, smooth, warm, damp. *What should I do?* He'd been down this path once before: a beautiful woman in tears, sex. It had left his life in ruins.

But Merry was no seductress. She was forthright and honest and nothing like Lavinia.

This wasn't a trick. It wasn't an attempt to manipulate him. Merry thought they were going to die, and she wanted to make love with him before that happened.

He knew what he *should* choose, knew what any honorable man should choose.

And he also knew that if he refused Merry, he would regret it as much as he regretted having sex with Lavinia.

BARNABY FOLDED BOTH blankets in half and laid them one on top of the other on the floor. It still wasn't nearly soft enough. *I can't do this.* His hair was stiff with grit. He was filthy. The blankets were too thin. He turned to her. "Merry . . ." *We can't.*

The words dried on his tongue.

They stared at one another for a long moment, both kneeling. Merry's expression was serious, solemn, and Barnaby had the feeling that she knew exactly what was going through his mind.

After an endless moment, she reached out and touched his cheek. "I love you."

"I love you, too," Barnaby whispered.

Merry put her arms around him and kissed him, a sweet, gentle kiss tasting of tears and lemonade. A kiss that left him feeling off balance. How had the tables turned? How was it that Merry was comforting *him,* and not the other way around? "It's all right, Barnaby," she whispered against his mouth.

They kissed, and kissed again—and there was warmth, but not heat. Barnaby couldn't find the passion he'd experienced earlier; he was too worried about what came next. She was a *virgin,* and he was *filthy,* and—

A sound like thunder came from the neighboring chamber. It rolled over them, crashing and booming, making them both flinch.

They broke apart and scrambled to their feet. Barnaby pressed Merry back against the wall, shielding her with his body. For a long, frightening moment, the clatter of falling rock reverberated around them, then it faded to silence. A puff of dust issued from the next cave.

"Stay here." Barnaby picked up the lantern. "I'll take a look."

"Barnaby . . ." Merry clutched his arm.

"I'll be careful." He bent, placed a kiss on her brow, and loosened her grip on his sleeve. "Don't worry."

He peered into the next cave, and stepped cautiously through. It didn't look as if much of the roof had come down; the rubble littering the floor was mostly small stones.

"Anyone hurt?" he called in a low voice.

No reply came.

His chest clutched faintly. He sent up a prayer: *Please God, don't let anyone be dead.*

Barnaby raised the lantern and peered at the debris above the giant's gravestone. "Anyone hurt?" he called again, a little more loudly.

Still no reply came, and now he saw why. The rabbit-sized hole was gone. There was no gap at all between this cave and the next.

Barnaby's chest clutched again, more strongly, and he experienced a faint sensation of panic—and then common sense prevailed. It didn't matter whether the hole was there or not; they weren't going to run out of air. Not for a long time. And it didn't matter if they couldn't communicate with the men on the other side of the rockfall. Communication or not, the excavation would continue unabated, the gap would be reopened, and they'd be rescued. He *knew* those for facts. Therefore, there was no reason to panic.

That logic worked for the front part of his brain, but not the back. At the very back of his brain, panic dug its claws in and told him that he and Merry were going to die.

Barnaby took a deep breath, fixed a smile on his face, and stepped back into the grotto.

Merry was standing exactly where he'd left her, hugging her

arms. Her eyes were huge in her pale face.

Barnaby stared at her, and tried to find a light quip, something to reassure her, but all he could think of was that Merry was right. This might be all the time they had.

So don't waste it.

He crossed to her, and put the lantern down, and took her in his arms. "It's not as bad as it sounded."

Merry hugged him back tightly, almost desperately.

Barnaby bent his head, and pressed his mouth to her dusty hair. "We're going to get out of here. I promise."

"You can't promise that," she whispered. "No one can promise that."

"I do promise it," Barnaby said firmly, and then he tilted up her chin and smiled at her, and said, "We *are* getting out of here," and he kissed Merry as she deserved to be kissed, wholeheartedly, with no doubt, no hesitation, no holding back.

He kissed her, and swung her up in his arms and laid her on the blankets, and kissed her again, losing himself in her mouth, while the warmth between them flared into heat, and the panic loosened its claws and faded away, and all that was left was sensation and a hot, urgent throb in his blood.

He nipped Merry's earlobe, laid burning kisses down her throat, fumbled open the buttons at the nape of her neck, baring the curve where her throat met her shoulder, and kissed her there, fierce, hungry kisses, using his tongue, using his teeth.

Barnaby yanked open more buttons, loosened the drawstring of her chemise, and was confronted by the creamy swell of Merry's upper breasts. He lost his breath for a moment. Such plump, enticing curves. He bent his head and laid a trembling, reverent kiss on that exposed skin. Smooth and soft and smelling of woman.

He groaned, low in his throat, and his trembling reverence fell away. His next kiss was hot and greedy, tasting as much of her as he could, exploring with his lips, his tongue—but Merry's nipples were just beyond reach and the damned corset was in the way.

Barnaby reached behind her and yanked at the laces, not thinking about propriety or respectability, letting the heat blur his thoughts. The corset opened half a dozen inches before the laces snared in a knot, but it was enough, because once he'd pushed the chemise out of the way, there were her nipples, pink and taut.

The air squeezed out of his lungs. God, her breasts were perfect. Perfect, and beautiful, and absolutely begging to be kissed.

He drew in a ragged breath, and bent to this task. Hungry kisses that made Merry gasp and arch closer. Her fingers buried themselves in his hair. She choked out his name.

Barnaby kissed her breasts, while the heat rose in him until he could barely think. His thoughts lurched in his skull as if he were drunk. Drunk on Merry's taste, on her scent, on the eager, breathless noises she was making.

He tore his mouth from her skin and gulped several ragged breaths. His pulse pounded in his head. He felt hot enough to asphyxiate.

Barnaby sat up and wrenched off his coat, ripped off his neckcloth. It became easier to breathe, easier to think. He inhaled several deep breaths, staring at Merry, at her rosy lips and flushed cheeks, at her bare throat, at the delicate line of her collarbone, at her pale, round breasts nestled in her corset, the pink nipples peeking at him.

But it wasn't her breasts that captured his attention, it was her eyes, dark in the candlelight. Barnaby gazed into her eyes, and felt his heart clench painfully in his chest. *I love you.* He reached out and touched one soft cheek with trembling fingers, then bent his head and kissed her, losing himself in the perfection of her mouth.

Heat built between them. Barnaby came up for air, eased one thigh between her legs, bent his head and found her mouth again, kissed her, rocked against her.

"Oh," Merry gasped.

Barnaby laughed into her mouth, and rocked again, and again, settling into a rhythm. Heat grew in him, flushing from his toes to his scalp. He kissed her more deeply, more urgently.

Time dissolved. He had no sense of how long they kissed for. His weight was half on her, his leg nestled between hers, and she was clutching him tightly, pressing back, and the rhythm between them became faster and faster . . .

Merry trembled beneath him and caught her breath.

Barnaby kept rocking, while Merry gasped and shuddered and clung to him. When her grip eased and her body relaxed, he let the rhythm stop. Blood pounded in his head. He dragged air into his lungs. "We can leave it at that," he said breathlessly.

To his relief, Merry said, "No."

Barnaby rolled his weight off her. His cock was painfully hard, pressing against his breeches. He reached for the hem of Merry's gown and drew it up her legs, exposing slender, shapely calves clad in white knit stockings.

Slow, slow.

He released his breath in a trickle, and bent his head and found her lips, kissing her gently while his hand slid up one leg, past the garter, to the silky skin of her inner thigh. Only the fastest of young ladies wore drawers. Merry wasn't one of them; his hand slid across warm, smooth, bare skin, higher, higher, to the thatch of hair at the junction of her thighs.

Merry tensed slightly. Barnaby stopped kissing her. "Relax," he whispered against her mouth.

They lay quietly in the almost-dark, lips touching, while he slowly explored her, finding the sensitive pearl of flesh, stroking it with his thumb, making her tremble. "Like that?"

"Yes," Merry whispered shyly.

Barnaby slid his forefinger inside her. She was slippery with juices. "Does that hurt?"

"No."

He stroked her with his thumb, and slid a second finger inside her, and stroked again. He didn't need to ask Merry whether she liked it. Her breathing was ragged. She pressed herself against his hand.

He kissed her, and she clutched his shirt and kissed him back, her inner muscles contracting around his fingers in a rhythm that made his cock strain against his breeches.

But when he inserted a third finger, Merry stiffened.

"It hurts?"

"A little."

Barnaby tried to steady his breathing, but his lungs had forgotten how to function properly. Each breath was a shallow gasp. "It'll hurt worse than this," he told her hoarsely.

"I don't care."

Barnaby hesitated for a long moment, and then slid his fingers from her and sat up. He unbuttoned his breeches. "Are you certain about this?" *Because once I start, I'm afraid I won't be able to stop.* It was two and a half years since he'd last had sex. Two and a half long years.

"I'm certain."

Barnaby unfastened his drawers. His cock sprang out. Moisture already dewed its tip. He inhaled a shallow breath and prayed for self-control.

He lay down again, and gently drew Merry's gown and petticoat and chemise up to her waist, and settled himself between her legs. "Are you certain?" he whispered, one last time.

"Yes."

Merry's gaze was direct. He found he couldn't look away. He had a sense that she was staring into his soul, that he was laid utterly bare to her, that she saw who he was, saw his fears, his regrets, his most shameful secrets—that she saw those things, and trusted him. Trusted him utterly.

Emotion welled in his chest. He bent his head and laid a kiss on her brow, a wordless declaration of love, and entered her as gently as he could.

Merry stiffened. Her breath caught in her throat.

Barnaby held himself still. Utterly and absolutely still. Rigidly still. His heart labored and his lungs labored and his muscles trembled with effort . . . and then Merry let out a slow breath and relaxed. "It's all right," she whispered, touching his cheek lightly. "It just burns a bit. Don't stop."

"Sure?" It was a rough, hoarse syllable.

"Yes."

He withdrew slightly and slid into her again. This time, Merry didn't tense.

Barnaby fell into a slow, gentle rhythm. It didn't matter what his body wanted, this was for Merry. Slow and gentle. Slow and gentle. His awareness of time faded. Minutes passed, or was it hours? Gradually, the pace he set quickened—and then quickened again—and then they were both panting, and Merry was no longer relaxed, but gripping his arms, arching against him—and then she shuddered, and he shuddered too, and his climax spilled through him, great convulsions of pleasure that went on without end, his muscles helplessly contracting and releasing until he was wholly spent.

Barnaby rolled to his side, holding Merry tightly. He held her while their breathing slowed, while their pulses steadied, while their skin cooled. Finally, reluctantly, he released her. He restored their clothing to order, relacing the corset, buttoning Merry's gown, and all the while, he found himself unable to speak. He had no words to express how he felt, the fierce, tender, utterly consuming love, the wonder.

He shrugged into his coat and stuffed the filthy neckcloth in a pocket. Merry watched him. Her expression was shy and solemn and joyful at the same time. He saw trust in her eyes. Pure, heart-stopping trust.

Barnaby stared at her for a long, long moment. Lavinia had destroyed him; Merry had restored him to himself. *This is how a phoenix feels, rising from the ashes.*

He reached out and touched her cheek with light fingers. *How did I deserve this?*

Merry laid her hand over his. "Thank you."

Emotion choked his throat. Barnaby shook his head. *No, thank you.*

CHAPTER SIXTEEN

THE GROTTO WAS as black as the inside of a tomb when Barnaby woke. He fumbled for the tinderbox, lit a fresh candle, and placed it in the lantern. God, what time was it? He felt as if three decades had passed while he slept. His bones ached as if he were an old man.

His pocket watch told him it was midday.

Barnaby rubbed his face. Stubble rasped under his hands. A bath and a shave. Those were what he wanted most when they got out of here: a bath and a shave.

If they got out of here.

He looked at Merry, half-hidden in the nest of blankets. Asleep, she looked like a child. A rush of tenderness tightened his throat. Carefully, he tucked the blankets around her. Viscount's granddaughter. Dancing master's daughter. *My wife.*

Merry was right; they did suit each other.

We will dance every day, and laugh every day, and be happy, he promised her silently.

Barnaby stood stiffly. He could feel every bruise he'd gathered yesterday. He picked up the lantern and tiptoed across to peer into the next cave. The scene was unchanged: the great, tilted slab, the rubble on the floor, the blocked gap.

No, there had been a change. The gap was no longer entirely blocked. There was a small hole to the left, as if a mole had burrowed through.

Barnaby gazed at that hole for a long moment, and released his breath. *We will get out of here.*

HE WASHED HIS face as best he could, and set out a sparse picnic, and woke Merry. After they'd eaten, Barnaby checked the gap again. The hole had grown to badger-size. If he held his breath and listened carefully, he heard muffled voices and the occasional *chink* of stone on stone.

By two o'clock the hole was as large as the one he and Sawyer had excavated. "Not long now," he told Merry. But two o'clock became three o'clock, and Barnaby found himself increasingly edgy. He wanted Merry out of here. He wanted her safe and above ground. He wanted it *now*. "Let's dance," he suggested, before his edginess could become full-blown agitation.

At three thirty, while they were practicing the waltz, Lady Cosgrove returned. Barnaby didn't see her arrive, but he saw the monkey sitting on the hamper.

"Charlotte!" Merry cried.

Barnaby retreated to the cave with the fossilized skeleton, so Lady Cosgrove could don her discarded clothing. He squatted alongside the skeleton and wished once again that he had a sketch pad and pencil. "I wonder what you were when you were alive? I wonder *when* you were alive?" He told the skeleton about the monkey that was actually Lady Cosgrove, and how Merry's birthday was tomorrow, and she'd be visited by a Faerie godmother, and how she'd choose a magical gift, too. "Preposterous, don't you think? And yet it's all true. I saw the monkey with my own eyes."

After fifteen minutes, he returned to the grotto.

"They're shoring it with timber," Lady Cosgrove said, fastening her nankeen boots. "Marcus says it won't be long now."

"He's not helping, is he?" Barnaby said, alarmed.

"Sawyer won't let him. He dragged Marcus back once in some kind of wrestling hold, and refuses to let him get close again. He says he promised you he'd keep Marcus out of danger."

Barnaby nodded.

"Marcus is *so* cross with you about that." Lady Cosgrove climbed to her feet, and stood on tiptoe, and kissed his bristly cheek. "But I'm not. Thank you."

"Has anyone been hurt? There was a devil of a rockfall this morning."

"No. Although I understand it was a close call." She ran her fingers through her messy hair. "Do I look dirty enough? I didn't have a bath."

"You look as dirty as me," Merry said. "But neither of us is a patch on Barnaby."

Both ladies turned to examine him. Lady Cosgrove's gaze took in his stiff hair, his stubbled face, his ripped coat and grimy breeches and scarred boots, before returning to his hair again. Barnaby resisted the urge to comb it with his fingers. He felt a blush creep beneath the stubble.

Lady Cosgrove grinned. "You would make a superb scarecrow."

BY FOUR THIRTY, the gap was pronounced safe. Rudkin, the young groom, whispered instructions from the top of the slab. He looked almost as much a scarecrow as Barnaby. "His lordship says to take it one at a time. Quiet and slow, like."

Lady Cosgrove wanted Merry to go first. "I've been gone the whole night and most of the day," she hissed in an undertone, but Merry flatly refused.

"You have a child; I don't."

Lady Cosgrove gave in, and climbed the rope ladder and crawled through the timber-shored gap. Rudkin waited a long moment, then beckoned to Merry.

Merry took a deep breath.

"It's perfectly safe," Barnaby told her. "Just take it slowly." And then—regardless of Rudkin watching them—he bent and kissed her.

Merry clutched him for several seconds, then pushed herself away and picked her way across the rock-strewn floor.

Barnaby watched her, almost afraid to breathe. He realized that he'd never understood fear before. *This* was true fear, this rib-squeezing, throat-choking emotion. He had the oddest sensation that his future had narrowed to a thin, fragile thread, and that the thread was about to snap, and when it snapped the whole world would collapse around his ears.

Merry climbed the rope ladder with quick agility and crawled out of sight through the gap.

The roof didn't fall.

Barnaby released the breath he'd been holding. His future seemed suddenly to balloon, as wide as the oceans.

Rudkin beckoned to him.

Barnaby picked up the hamper and blankets and repeated Merry's climb, just as silently, but less nimbly. He passed the blankets to Rudkin, and then the hamper, and hauled himself up onto the slab, half-afraid their combined weight would make it shift again.

It didn't.

He crawled through the gap, glad of the boards holding the roof up, and blinked with astonishment. The men had been busy. The rockfall was almost entirely cleared, right down to the floor, and in place of the rubble was a rough barricade of wood. Planks and timbers were jammed every which way and braced with great beams. No wonder the giant slab hadn't moved; half a forest was holding it in place.

A six-rung wooden ladder was propped up for him to climb down, held by a gardener, and in the larger cavern beyond, he saw the shadowy figures of at least half a dozen people. His eyes picked out Marcus and Sawyer and Lady Cosgrove. And Merry. Merry, safe and unharmed.

A sense of lightness came, as if wings had sprouted from his shoulders and he was hovering in the air.

Barnaby reached back for the hamper and handed it to the gardener, then tossed the blankets down. "After you," he told Rudkin.

"Master says we're to bring the rope ladder. He wants no one else coming here."

Barnaby helped the groom haul the rope ladder up. "You go first. I'll hand it down to you."

"Yes, sir." Rudkin scrambled down the ladder.

Barnaby dropped the bulky bundle to him, then climbed down himself. When his feet touched the ground, the sensation of lightness became even stronger. He was so buoyant that surely he was floating. He turned and looked up at the gap, at the wedged-in timbers, at the dark cavity where the roof had fallen.

There was a sharp *crack* of splintering wood. Everything went black.

CHAPTER SEVENTEEN

April 12th, 1807
Devonshire

WHEN MERRY WAS a child, it had sometimes seemed that her birthday would never dawn. She had the same feeling now, as if time crept past at glacial speed. She stared at the walnut and gold spring-clock on her mantelpiece, and watched the minute hand move another grudging increment. Distantly, the great longcase clock in the entrance hall struck five times.

Another hour gone. Was Barnaby still alive?

Merry took up her chamberstick, let herself out of her room, and hurried down the dark, silent corridor. The servants weren't yet up.

She quietly opened the door to the blue bedchamber. A fire burned in the grate and candles blazed in the sconces.

The servants weren't awake, but Marcus was, sitting vigil at Barnaby's bedside. He looked drawn and tired, and more than that, he looked like a man who had lost hope.

"Any change?" she whispered.

Marcus shook his head.

But there had been a change. Merry saw it as soon as she stepped close to the big four-poster bed. Barnaby's skin tone was grayer, and a blue tinge had come to his lips.

Her heart kicked in her chest—*he's dead*—and she reached

for his wrist. No, not dead. Not yet. Her fingers found a faint, thready pulse. His skin was cold, though, despite the warmth of the room, and when she bent close, she barely heard him breathe.

Merry released Barnaby's wrist and gazed down at him. The shape of his face was wrong—that dreadful lump on his forehead, the lopsided jaw. His eyelids were purple and swollen. It was as if a monster's face had been grafted to Barnaby's skull, all distorted features and discolored skin.

"He'll be fine," she told Marcus, with a confidence she didn't feel. "I'll heal him, just as soon as Baletongue comes."

Marcus didn't say anything. His expression didn't alter. He knew as well as she did that they were running out of time.

DAWN CAME, AND Woodhuish Abbey woke around her—Merry heard the creak of footsteps, the murmur of distant voices. She stayed in her bedchamber; Baletongue would only come if she was alone.

A housemaid brought her a breakfast she couldn't eat, and an hour later removed it.

Merry sat at her little escritoire, the list of Faerie gifts spread out before her, and waited. And waited. The clock hands inched around the enamel dial, and the sense of time running out became stronger and stronger until she could barely breathe.

Another hour crept past. Merry read the list for the thousandth time. After *Finding People and/or Objects,* but before *Invisibility* and *Levitation,* were several different types of healing. Healing fevers. Healing illnesses of the mind. Healing physical traumata. *Note that a healer gives of her own strength with each healing,* someone had written in crabbed, old-fashioned writing. *Only women in the most robust of health should consider requesting these gifts.*

A shiver ran up the back of Merry's neck. She jerked her head around and half-rose from the chair. "Hello?"

Her room was utterly empty, utterly silent—and yet a prickling sensation crept from the base of Merry's spine all the way to her scalp. She knew what it meant: Baletongue was here. Her gaze jumped to the clock. Ten o'clock. "Hello?" she said more urgently. "Show yourself."

A patch of air in the corner of the chamber shimmered like a heat haze—and between one blink of Merry's eyes and the next, a woman came into being.

She looked as if she had stepped from an Elizabethan painting: the blood-red velvet gown, the lace ruff, the dark hair elaborately dressed with pearls.

Merry stared. Baletongue was inhumanly beautiful, her features cold and chiseled and perfect. But most inhuman of all were her eyes. They had no white sclera, no colored iris. They were purely black.

Merry discovered that her heart was beating fast and high at the base of her throat.

"Anne Ignatia Merryweather?"

Merry swallowed. "Yes. Good morning." Her voice came out higher than normal.

Baletongue didn't return the greeting. She stared at Merry scornfully, and there was such malice in those black eyes that Merry's urgent words dried on her tongue. She understood her mother's warning. *Treat her with utmost caution. She delights in doing harm.*

Merry swallowed again, and found her voice. "I would like to choose a healing gift. I understand that I may choose a single act of healing, performed by you, or I can choose to become a healer myself and heal numerous people."

Baletongue stared coldly at her.

The safest choice would be to request that Baletongue heal

Barnaby. There could be no doubt then that he would survive. But what about the groom, Rudkin, with his right shin smashed to smithereens?

"Can you please explain this particular gift to me?" Merry picked up the list and found the item she wanted. "Healing physical traumata."

Baletongue stared at her without replying.

Merry's temper sparked. "If I choose this gift, exactly what traumata may I heal?" she demanded. "Injuries to bones, as well as injuries to the flesh?"

"Correct." Baletongue's tone was dismissive, disdainful.

"And how do I do it? How does one heal?"

"When you lay your hands on the patient, you will understand what needs doing. As to whether you can do it or not . . ." Baletongue's upper lip curled contemptuously. "That depends on your strength and your willpower."

"There's a man, three rooms from here." Merry gripped the list tightly. "His skull is broken. And his jaw. If I choose this gift, will I be able to save his life?"

Baletongue's gaze shifted fractionally. She was silent for a long moment, and then she blinked, and her pale lips curved upwards. "It's more than just his skull and jaw."

"Can I save his life with this gift?" Merry cried urgently.

Baletongue's lips twitched in amusement. "You'd have to hurry."

"I take the gift. Now."

Baletongue smiled, showing foxlike white teeth. "Done." A snap of her fingers, a heat shimmer in the air, and she was gone.

Merry dropped the list and ran, wrenching open her door, spilling out into the corridor. Now the seconds were dashing past too fast. *Hurry. Hurry!*

She jerked open the door to Barnaby's room so hard it slammed against the wall.

Marcus recoiled out of his chair. "Jesus—" And then he took in her expression. "She came?"

"She came."

Merry hurried to the bed and placed her hands on Barnaby's head. His hair was stiff with dust and blood.

For a moment, nothing happened . . . and then awareness flowed through her hands. She had no word for it—intuition, knowledge, insight—but whatever it was, it told her exactly what Barnaby's injuries were. Baletongue had been correct; it was more than just his skull and jaw.

"His neck's broken, too."

"His neck?" Marcus said, aghast. "Christ, Merry!"

"I can fix it," Merry said. Strength and willpower, Baletongue had said. And she had both of those.

She hastily dragged Marcus's chair closer to the bed and sat. "Keep everyone out, except you and Charlotte."

"The doctor—"

"Especially the doctor." Merry took Barnaby's limp right hand in both of hers.

"He's here now," Marcus said. "He's talking of amputating Rudkin's leg."

"Amputating?" Her head jerked around.

"He says it's too badly broken to heal."

"For God's sake, don't let him!"

The tension in Marcus's face eased fractionally. "I won't."

Merry turned back to Barnaby and bent her attention fiercely to him. She didn't notice Marcus leave the room and quietly close the door.

BALETONGUE HAD SAID that she would know what to do, and she did. It was simply a matter of *requiring* certain actions to occur—bones mended, torn muscles repaired, accumulated fluid redirected. Requiring the action caused it to happen.

Merry worked methodically. Her gift told her which were the most urgent actions, and she attended to them first. But there were *dozens* of urgent actions. And scores of less urgent actions. And each action took effort and focus and time. Edges of bones didn't instantly bond, nor did swelling subside and severed nerves knit together; it was a slow, creeping process, and she had to concentrate hard while it happened, had to *will* it to happen, or it didn't.

She was vaguely aware of Charlotte and Marcus slipping in and out of the bedchamber. Refreshments were placed within reach, teapots refilled, the fire banked.

The healing went on—and on—and on. Bones and blood vessels. Muscles and nerves. Repair after repair after repair, until at last her magic told her there was nothing more to be done. Merry released Barnaby's hand and sat back in the chair, feeling stiff, tired, hungry, and a little light-headed.

"How's it going?" a quiet voice asked.

Merry jumped slightly. She hadn't realized Charlotte was in the room. "He's healed. But his body needs rest. It'll be hours before he wakes." She yawned.

Charlotte poured her a cup of tea and held it out. "Hungry?"

"Starving." Merry looked at the clock, and blinked. Had she been sitting here for *eight* hours?

Charlotte picked up a tray that was sitting on the hearth, and placed it on the table beside Merry. There was a little silver soup tureen, and a covered plate. The smell of roasted meat made Merry's mouth water. She lifted the gleaming tureen lid. "How's Rudkin?"

"In considerable pain."

Merry met her eyes. "Bad?"

Charlotte grimaced. "We're keeping him sedated with laudanum. When he's awake, he cries."

Merry lost her appetite. She replaced the lid. "I'll see him now."

CHAPTER EIGHTEEN

HUNGER WOKE HER at two in the morning, despite the huge supper she'd eaten. Fortunately, Charlotte had left a bowl of fruit and a dish of shelled nuts on the bedside table.

Merry ate a pear, two handfuls of nuts, and a bunch of grapes, snuggled drowsily beneath the covers again—and thought of Barnaby. Had he yet woken?

Her weariness vanished. Anxiety took its place.

Merry flung back the covers, took up her chamberstick, hurried from her room and down the dark corridor.

Sir Barnaby's door opened on silent hinges. His bedchamber was dark. Marcus was no longer on vigil.

Merry trod softly across to the big four-posted bed.

Candlelight showed her Barnaby asleep, curled up on his side, his face utterly relaxed. A tray sat on his bedside table. She saw a bunch of grapes like the one she'd just eaten, a jug of lemonade, and a plate bearing two of Guillaume's incomparable pastries. From the appearance of the plate, at least three more pastries had once sat on it.

Her anxious tension eased. Barnaby must have woken. Woken, and eaten, and convinced Marcus that he was well enough to be left alone.

Merry tiptoed closer and gazed down at him.

Not only woken and eaten, but bathed and shaved, too. His

red-brown hair was no longer filthy, the whiskers were gone from his skin, and he wore a clean nightshirt.

She lightly touched his brow, trying to sense his wellness.

Barnaby's eyes opened. He blinked drowsily. "Merry?"

Merry curled her hand into her chest. "I'm sorry," she whispered. "I didn't mean to wake you. Go back to sleep."

Sir Barnaby pushed up on one elbow and rubbed his face. "How do you feel?"

"Fine." He sat fully upright and rubbed his face again, rubbed his hair. "How are you?"

"Me? I'm perfectly well."

Barnaby fixed her with a frowning stare. "Marcus says my neck was broken. And my head."

Merry nodded.

"He says you saved my life."

Merry nodded again.

"Thank you." Barnaby gave her a faint, lopsided smile, and held out his hand.

Merry took it.

Barnaby's fingers gripped hers tightly. "Thank you," he said, a second time.

Merry stared into his hazel eyes, and felt emotion clench in her chest. *I love this man.*

Barnaby's stomach gave a small growl. "Sorry," he said, ruefully. "I'm hungry."

BARNABY ATE THE bunch of grapes and one of Guillaume's pastries. He offered her the second pastry. Merry shook her head. Barnaby ate that pastry, too, and drank some lemonade. He offered her the glass. Merry sipped, sitting cross-legged beside him on the bed. The lemonade was tart and refreshing, and the taste reminded her of the grotto, reminded her of darkness and shyness and kissing Barnaby.

She wasn't shy with him now. She felt comfortable and at ease and happy. Profoundly happy.

Barnaby drank the last of the lemonade, put the glass on the side table, and sighed, a contented sound. His hazel eyes were heavy-lidded.

"Go to sleep," Merry told him.

"Soon." He put an arm around her shoulders, drew her close, and kissed her lightly.

Merry leaned into the kiss. Barnaby tasted of lemonade and chocolate.

They kissed once, sleepily, and a second time, less sleepily, and a third time, not sleepily at all. Barnaby drew back and looked at her. "Merry?"

Merry read the question on his face, and nodded.

"Are you certain?"

She nodded again.

Barnaby released her, and climbed out of bed, and locked the door. Then he came back and stood looking down at her. "This time we do it properly."

PROPERLY MEANT BEING naked. And it meant Barnaby kissing her from head to toe—quite literally. He kissed her jaw, her throat, kissed his way down one arm to her fingertips, and back up the other one. Then he turned his attention to her breasts. Long, exquisite minutes passed. He kissed lower—and lower— and then Merry lost the ability to think for a while. Pleasure built inside her until it overflowed. When coherent thought returned, Barnaby was kissing her ankle.

He came slowly back up her body—his mouth on her inner thigh, her midriff, the hollow of her collarbone—and found her lips again. Merry clutched him close and returned his kiss greedily. And then *she* got the chance to explore him, to trace the outline of muscle and bone in his shoulders, to test the warm pliancy of his skin with her tongue, with her teeth, to discover that he groaned when she tweaked his nipples, that he trembled when she ran her fingertips over his abdomen. She felt no shyness, just curiosity and wonder and joy. *I love this man.*

When she reached his groin, she halted, disconcerted by how different he was from her, uncertain how to proceed. She glanced at his face. "What's it called?"

"I call it my cock."

"May I touch it?"

"Do you want to?"

Now, the shyness came. Merry felt herself blush. She bit her lip, and nodded.

Barnaby sat up. He took her hand in his, and held her palm to his cock, wrapping her fingers around that strong, sturdy shaft.

His cock was hot. Burningly hot. It seemed to throb with urgency in her hand.

Merry's heart kicked in her chest, and began beating faster. She found herself growing short of breath. She glanced at Barnaby's face again—and her gaze was caught. His eyes, those hazel eyes, were somehow as hot and urgent as his cock nestled in her palm.

Her lungs forgot how to breathe. Her heart forgot how to beat.

They stared at each other while time slowed and seemed almost to stop—and then Merry tore her gaze from Barnaby's hot eyes, and looked down at her hand gripping him and saw a bead of moisture ease its way onto the plump, rosy crown of his cock.

"Enough," Barnaby said, his voice slightly hoarse, and he removed her hand.

"But I'm only halfway down you."

"You can do the other half when we're married." Barnaby

gathered her in his arms and rolled so that she lay beneath him.

Merry stopped protesting. Her entire body seemed to jolt with pleasure, with craving. This was what she wanted: *This*.

Barnaby settled himself between her legs. "Tell me if it hurts."

But it didn't hurt, didn't hurt at all, and it was a thousand times more marvelous than it had been in the grotto, because this time there were no clothes between them, and she wasn't afraid the ceiling was going to fall on their heads.

Sex was like dancing, Merry decided. Dancing to music that they heard in their blood, their bodies moving together in a rhythm that was primitive and powerful, the tempo rising, rising.

When the tempo reached *allegretto,* Merry stopped thinking about dancing. Her focus narrowed to sensation—the exhilarating friction of Barnaby's skin against hers, the physical heat building between them, the sound of panted breaths, the rapid thud of her heartbeat, the glorious flex of muscle each time she arched up to him.

And then the pleasure came again, waves of pleasure that crashed through her like waves crashing against the great cliffs of Woodhuish, and she cried out, and Barnaby cried out, too, and the waves tossed her high for a long, glorious moment, and then the waves slowly faded to ripples, and Merry was able to think again.

Sex was *much* better than dancing.

Barnaby gathered her in his arms and rolled so that she lay on him. He drew the rumpled bedclothes up, tucking them warmly around them both, and held her close. His cock still nestled inside her.

Merry rested her head on his chest and listened to his heart beating, more relaxed than she'd ever been in her life. Happier than she'd ever been in her life.

This man.

Barnaby's hand stroked down her back to her waist, and up again. "You fit very nicely here."

"Yes."

She thought of Henry—dead at twenty-six—and of her mother and father, dead, too—and felt the familiar grief, the familiar aching loss—and then she thought of Barnaby, who was alive, and whose heart beat slowly and steadily beneath her ear, and whose hand idly stroked her back—and relief welled inside her so strongly that tears came to her eyes. Barnaby hadn't died. Barnaby was alive.

While she was thinking of Barnaby, she drifted to sleep, pillowed on his chest. His voice drew her back to wakefulness. "Merry? Merry, love?" He gently shook her shoulder.

Merry rubbed her face, and reluctantly climbed off him. Barnaby looked as drowsy as she felt. He stifled a yawn, and groped on the floor for her nightgown.

Merry drew it over her head. The touch of cool linen on her skin made her shiver. She wanted nothing more than to stay in the warm, cozy nest of Barnaby's bed and fall asleep with him.

Barnaby swallowed another yawn, fumbled into his nightshirt, and picked up the chamberstick. The candle was half burned down.

He crossed to the door and unlocked it.

Merry reluctantly followed.

Barnaby bent to kiss her. "G'night."

Merry gazed up at him, at the tousled red-brown hair, the sleepy eyes, the bare throat above the open collar of his nightshirt. Her heart clenched in her chest. *I love you.* "Good night." She put her arms around him for a moment, and let his warmth sink into her body, let his scent fill her lungs. Barnaby. Who was alive. And then she took the chamberstick, tiptoed back down the dark corridor, crawled into her own bed, and slept for twelve straight hours.

CHAPTER NINETEEN

April 13th, 1807

April 13th, 1807
Devonshire

"I STILL DON'T remember a thing," Barnaby said, and it was extremely disconcerting to know that the roof literally *had* fallen on his head and he couldn't recall it.

"It's just as well." Marcus poured them both sherry from the decanters lined up on the oak sideboard. "Rudkin was screaming. I think the sound will live in my nightmares forever."

Barnaby accepted the glass Marcus held out to him. He crossed to the French doors that led to the terrace, and gazed out at the encroaching dusk. "How is Rudkin?"

Marcus came to stand beside him. "As spry as he ever was. Thanks to Merry." He raised his glass in a silent toast.

"And Doctor Curnow? What did he have to say about it all?"

"I don't think he knew *what* to say. He was remarkably silent. Dumbstruck."

Barnaby glanced at Marcus. "What did you tell him?"

"To consider it a miracle. Two miracles. And to please not discuss it with anyone. God only knows what he thinks."

"That it's magic," Barnaby said dryly. He sipped the sherry and gazed out the window, up the valley, towards Woodhuish House. He thought of the warm red brick and the whimsically twisting chimneys. "Merry said you haven't decided what you're going to do with Woodhuish House."

"Did she?" Marcus turned sideways and leaned his shoulders against the wall. "That's not exactly true. I had hoped . . . that you would like it."

Barnaby glanced at him. Marcus's expression wasn't quite as nonchalant as his posture. "I do like it."

"It's yours, if you wish. Yours and Merry's. Consider it a wedding gift."

Barnaby knew how the doctor had felt: dumbstruck. After a moment, he managed to say, "Merry told you?"

"She told Charlotte. Charlotte told me."

Barnaby stared out the window. Woodhuish House as a wedding gift? He didn't know what to say. Should he refuse? Accept? Insist on paying for it? Finally, he turned to Marcus and said, "Thank you."

Marcus nodded.

For a moment, he felt he should say more—protestations of gratitude, vows of everlasting friendship—and then he realized it wasn't necessary. Marcus understood.

Barnaby turned back to the window and took a sip of sherry. A peculiar sensation was growing beneath his breastbone, a sensation unlike anything he'd felt before, an odd mixture of contentment and excitement. He wasn't sure what to call it. A sense of looking forward to the future?

"There's a large farming estate three miles from here," Marcus said. "Been badly mismanaged. The owner's looking to sell."

"How badly mismanaged?"

"Very badly. It would be a challenge. But the right man could turn it around."

Their eyes met. Barnaby found himself grinning. "I'll ride over and look at it tomorrow."

Marcus nodded, and sipped his sherry. "Have you given

thought to Charles's christening?"

"Yes. I'd like to stand as his godfather."

"Good." Marcus's shoulders relaxed fractionally; that nonchalant pose had been even more fake than Barnaby had realized.

A sudden lump grew in his throat. "Marcus . . . you're my best friend."

Marcus surveyed him for several seconds, and then gave a small, slightly crooked smile.

Barnaby had been reading Marcus's smiles for thirty years. This smile said, *I know.* And it said, *You're my best friend, too.*

The lump in his throat grew bigger. He took a hasty gulp of sherry. Behind them, the door opened.

Marcus pushed away from the wall. "Merry."

Barnaby turned around sharply.

Merry stood on the far side of the drawing room, dressed for dinner in a gown the color of amethysts.

He stared at her. Merry. Merry of the astute eyes and sharp mind, who saw things no one else saw, and said things no one else would say. Vibrant, forthright, unconventional Merry. Merry who ran down hills like a young girl. Merry who loved to dance and to laugh. Merry, who had saved his life in more ways than one. *His* Merry.

"I'll see where Charlotte is," Marcus murmured, put down his glass, and slid from the room.

Barnaby put his own glass down blindly and took a step towards Merry. Her eyes met his, a dimple peeked in one cheek— and then they were both in the middle of the drawing room, and her arms were around his neck, and he swung her up and held her very, very, *very* tightly.

A long moment passed, during which he stood with his eyes closed, drinking in the sheer wonderfulness of holding her—her warm body, her faint floral scent, her soft hair tickling his jaw.

"You slept a long time. Are you all right?"

"Perfectly. You?"

Barnaby set Merry on her feet and examined her face. "I've never been better." *Thanks to you.* But for Merry, he'd have turned around before he ever got to Woodhuish.

She hadn't merely given him his life, she'd given him his *life*.

He touched her cheek, where the dimple quivered. "When shall we get married? Would you like the banns read, or a special license?"

"Special license," Merry said firmly. "Next week. Unless . . . you want to wait?"

Barnaby shook his head. "The sooner, the better."

And then he laughed, and swung Merry up in his arms again, and kissed her joyfully.

AUTHOR'S NOTE

I CONFESS TO taking some liberties with geography. Although Woodhuish *does* lie on the southeast Devon coast, Woodhuish Abbey is actually based on Hartland Abbey, in northwest Devon, with its gothic façade and walled gardens. And my Woodhuish has many more trees than the real Woodhuish.

Woodhuish House is reminiscent of Mapledurham House, which is in Oxfordshire, rather a long way from Devon. The Tudor brick chimneys look *extremely* similar to those at Hampton Court Palace, in Richmond upon Thames.

The cave system is loosely based on Kents Cavern in Torquay, about ten miles north of Woodhuish. (At the time this story is set, it was known as Kent's Hole.) Roman coins were found in Kents Cavern, as were the remains of cave bears, cave lions, saber-toothed cats, wolves, cave hyenas, wooly rhinos, and mammoths. I like to think that Marcus would allow members of the Linnean Society access to the Woodhuish caves, and that similar items might be discovered there.

THANK YOU

Thanks for reading *Resisting Miss Merryweather*. I hope you enjoyed it!

If you'd like to be notified when I release new books, please join my Readers' Group (www.emilylarkin.com/newsletter).

I welcome all honest reviews. Reviews and word of mouth help other readers to find books, so please consider taking a few moments to leave a review on Goodreads or elsewhere.

Resisting Miss Merryweather is the second book in the Baleful Godmother series. The first is *Unmasking Miss Appleby,* and the subsequent ones are *Trusting Miss Trentham, Claiming Mister Kemp, Ruining Miss Wrotham,* and *Discovering Miss Dalrymple,* with more to follow. I hope you enjoy them all!

Those of you who like to start a series at its absolute beginning may wish to read the series prequel—the Fey Quartet—a quartet of novellas that tell the tales of a widow, her three daughters, and one baleful Faerie. Their titles are *Maythorn's Wish, Hazel's Promise, Ivy's Choice,* and *Larkspur's Quest.* A free digital copy of *The Fey Quartet* is available to anyone who joins my Readers' Group. Visit www.emilylarkin.com/starter-library.

If you'd like to read the first chapter of *Trusting Miss Trentham,* the next novel in the Baleful Godmother series, please turn the page.

CHAPTER ONE

October 31ˢᵗ, 1808
London

Miss Letitia Trentham, England's wealthiest unmarried heiress, received her eighteenth proposal of the year at the Hammonds' ball. The Little Season was drawing to its close and the company was thin, but more than a hundred people crowded the ballroom. Four of them were currently angling after her fortune.

When Laurence Darlington suggested that they sit out their next dance, Letty experienced a sinking feeling. When Darlington suggested that they repair to the conservatory, the sinking feeling became stronger. The conservatory adjoined the ballroom—was in fact in full view of the ballroom, had a table of refreshments and an attendant footman, and could hardly be called secluded—but it was secluded enough for a proposal.

Experience had taught Letty that it was better to get proposals over with as swiftly as possible, so she let Darlington lead her down the short flight of marble stairs.

The musicians struck the first notes of a *contredanse.* "Champagne?" offered the footman.

Yes, a big glass, Letty thought. "No, thank you."

Laurence Darlington led her to the farthest end of the conservatory, where there was a stiff array of ferns and a row of gilded chairs precisely aligned. Only a glimpse of the ballroom could be seen. Music floated down the steps. The smell of the ball—sweet perfumes, spicy pomades, and pungent sweat—smothered any scent of greenery.

Letty sat and smoothed the sea-green silk of her ball gown over her knees and braced herself for what was to come. For the past two weeks, Laurence Darlington had been doing a good impression of a man falling in love. It was one of the better impressions she'd seen this year, although not as good as Sir Charles Stanton's. *That* had been masterful.

Laurence Darlington sat alongside her and gazed ardently into her eyes. A very handsome man, Darlington. The most handsome of this year's crop of fortune hunters. And up to his ears in debt.

"Miss Trentham," Darlington said, emotion throbbing in his voice. "What I am about to say can surely come as no surprise to you."

No. No surprise.

Letty heard the proposal with weary resignation. It was a pretty speech. Darlington wasn't fool enough to call her beautiful; instead, he praised her character and her intelligence. Even so, his words resonated with falsehood. When he finished, he said passionately, "There is no one I would rather marry. No one! You are everything I could ever wish for in a wife." The first half of that statement rang with a clear, bell-like tone. It was actually the truth. The second half gave a discordant *clang* in Letty's ears.

"I lay my heart at your feet."

Darlington was a good actor. He did almost look like a man who'd laid his heart at his lover's feet. His handsome face bore an expression of hopeful longing and his eyes burned with passion.

Passion for my fortune.

"You love me, Mr. Darlington?"

"Yes," Darlington said fervently.

"And my fortune . . . ?"

"Means nothing to me!"

Darlington's delivery was perfect—the earnest expression, the vehement tone. Letty might have believed him, if not for the dissonant *clang* in her ears, like a cracked church bell being struck. She took a moment to be thankful that she had a Faerie godmother, that she'd been given a wish on her twenty-first birthday and that she'd wished as she had, that she *could* hear Darlington's lies.

"Tell me, Mr. Darlington, if we married, would you be faithful?"

Darlington blinked. He hadn't expected that question. None of her suitors ever did. But she always asked it. "Of course!"

Clang.

Letty nodded, as if she believed him. She looked down at her hands and smoothed a wrinkle in one of her gloves. "Is it true that you're a gambler, Mr. Darlington?"

Darlington appeared not to have expected this question either. There was a short pause, and then he said lightly, "I roll the dice occasionally."

Letty glanced at him. More than occasionally, and more than just dice. Cards. Horses. Dogfights. Cockfights. Prizefights. Anything and everything, if what she'd heard was correct.

"And is it true that you're almost bankrupt?"

It was a shockingly rude question to ask, one she wouldn't have asked in her first season, or even her third, but years of fortune hunters had taught her that bluntness was best.

Darlington stiffened. The mask of passionate lover slipped slightly. His smile was fixed, almost a grimace.

They stared at each other for a long moment, while the strains of the *contredanse* drifted down from the ballroom, and then

Darlington relaxed and laughed. "My dear Miss Trentham, I can assure you that—"

"I sympathize with your financial troubles, Mr. Darlington," Letty said brusquely. "But I will not marry you."

Darlington lost his smile. He closed his mouth. The glitter in his eyes wasn't passion. Color rose in his cheeks. Not embarrassment, but anger.

His jaw tightened. He stood stiffly and turned from her without speaking, strode across the marble floor, climbed the shallow steps to the ballroom.

Letty watched him disappear among the dancers. Fury surged through her, fierce and bitter. How dare he? How dare any man pretend a love he didn't feel and vow a fidelity he had no intention of keeping?

On the heels of fury was an urge to cry. Tears stung her eyes. Letty blinked them back. She would *not* cry over a man like Laurence Darlington. She wouldn't cry over *any* false suitor—a promise she'd made to herself in her first season.

But that promise was becoming harder to keep. The proposals had always hurt, but this year they hurt more than ever. This year, each proposal made her feel older and plainer and lonelier. Lonelier than she'd ever felt in her life. A hopeless, aching loneliness. And while part of that loneliness was because her cousin Julia had died last year, an equal part of it was because she was twenty-seven and still unmarried. *Will no one ever love me for myself?*

After all these years on the Marriage Mart and nearly two hundred proposals, it seemed unlikely.

I wish I weren't an heiress. For a brief moment, Letty indulged in a dream of going somewhere far, far away where no one knew who she was, and winning true love, like a princess dressed as a pauper in a Faerie tale.

She snorted under her breath. Princesses in Faerie tales were always beautiful, and she was most definitely *not* beautiful.

Perhaps that's what I should have wished for on my twenty-first birthday: Beauty, not hearing lies. But then she would have been a beautiful heiress, besieged by suitors and unable to hear their falsehoods—and *that* road must surely have led to misery.

"Miss Trentham?"

Letty glanced up. A man stood before her. He was tall, taller than Darlington, and broad in the shoulder. He was dressed for dancing in a tailcoat and knee breeches and silk stockings, but despite those clothes he looked as if he had no place at the Hammonds' ball. No languid tulip of the *ton*, this man. He was whipcord lean, his skin tanned brown, his expression unsmiling. He looked almost dangerous.

Letty felt a slight flare of nervousness. She looked for the footman. Yes, he still manned the refreshment table.

"Miss Trentham?" the man asked again. The tan gave a misleading impression of health. He wasn't just lean, he was gaunt. His tailcoat, for all its fine cut, hung on his frame.

A soldier back from India, invalided out? His dark brown hair was clipped short and his bearing was military.

"Yes."

"My name is Reid. I wondered if I might have a few words with you?" She saw exhaustion on his face, and tension.

Letty hesitated, wishing for the nominal chaperonage of Mrs. Sitwell, currently ensconced in the card room. *Get this over with, whatever it is.* "I'm engaged for the next dance, but until then you may certainly speak, Mr. Reid."

"Thank you." He gave a curt nod.

Letty folded her hands in her lap and gazed up at him, trying to look politely expectant, not nervous.

Mr. Reid gave her a long, frowning stare and then said abruptly, "You have a reputation for being able to distinguish truth from lies."

Letty tried not to stiffen. "Some people believe I can." She said it with a smile of amusement, as if she thought it a joke.

Mr. Reid didn't return the smile. "Can you?"

It wasn't the first time Letty had been asked this question. She'd learned to turn it aside with a jest, with a lie. But something about Mr. Reid made that impossible. His eyes were intent on her face. They were an extremely pale shade of gray, almost silver. She had an odd sense that his gaze was razor-sharp, penetrating skin and bone. Her awareness of him became even stronger—his tension, his exhaustion. *There is something very wrong with this man.*

"Sometimes," Letty said, and heard a *clang* in her ears at the lie. "Sit down, Mr. Reid. Tell me what it is you wish to know the truth of."

Reid hesitated, and then pulled one of the gilded chairs out of line and sat at an angle to her. He moved like a soldier—precise, controlled movements with no graceful flourishes.

Once seated, he was silent for several seconds, then spoke tersely: "There are two men here in London—I served with them in Portugal—one of them passed information to the French."

Letty blinked, hearing the truth in his words.

"I've spoken with them, and they both say they didn't, but *someone* did, and they were the only ones who knew other than the general and myself. The general didn't tell anyone. *I* didn't tell anyone. One of these two men lied, and I can't tell which one. Would you be able to?"

Letty released her breath slowly and sat back in her chair. "Perhaps." *Clang.* "If one of these men is a traitor, what will you do?"

"I don't know."

Clang.

"That, Mr. Reid, is a lie."

Hope flared in his silver eyes, flared on his gaunt face. He leaned forward. "You *can* tell."

"What will you do to him?" Letty repeated.

"Probably kill him." This time, Reid spoke the truth.

Tiny hairs pricked up on the back of Letty's neck. She glanced at the footman, stationed at the refreshment table, and back at Reid. Common sense urged her to push to her feet and walk from him as quickly as she could—run, if she had to. This man was *dangerous*, possibly even deranged.

Wary caution kept her where she was. "I need to know more before I decide whether I can help you."

Reid sat back in his chair, even tenser than he'd been before. "What do you want to know?"

"Everything."

He stared at her for a long moment, grim-faced, and then began to speak. "I was on General Wellesley's staff, an exploring officer. Reconnaissance. We'd been in Portugal less than a month. We engaged the French at Roliça, and then four days later at Vimeiro."

Letty nodded. She'd heard of the battles. Victories for England, both of them. "August of this year?"

"Yes." Reid's hands were clenched together, his knuckles sharp ridges beneath the gloves. "I had three local scouts. I went out daily with them. Not all together, you understand. I'd go with one man; the others would scout alone. We met each evening. On the day before Vimeiro, just on dusk, we were captured. The scouts were summarily executed."

Killed in front of him, was what he meant. Letty swallowed. "Why weren't you executed?"

"I was in uniform; they weren't."

She nodded.

"The French were waiting for us. It was an ambush. And *I* had chosen our meeting place. Other than the general, only two men knew of it. They both claim not to have told a soul—and yet one of them *must* have."

"Who are these men?"

"Wellesley's aides-de-camp."

Letty frowned. "Surely such men would be trustworthy?"

"Someone told the French," Reid said flatly. "It wasn't me, it wasn't the general, it wasn't my scouts."

Letty gazed at him uneasily. *Do I want to go further with this?* Reid's tension was disturbing. He seemed balanced on a knife-edge. *What if he kills a man based on my say-so?*

She opened her mouth to tell him that her rumored ability to distinguish truth from lies was merely a trick, that she'd only guessed he was lying earlier—and then closed it again.

What if she *didn't* help Reid, and he killed the wrong man?

Letty chewed on this thought for a moment, and then said, "Tell me about the two men, Mr. Reid."

"They were new. I didn't know them well. Didn't like them much. Playing at soldiering." His upper lip curled. "Wellesley didn't like them either. They'd been foisted on him."

Letty raised her brows. "You didn't know these men well, and yet you told them where you and your scouts would be?"

"Wellesley had asked me to keep him informed of my movements. He was in a meeting when I left, so I told his aides."

"And both these men are currently in London?"

Reid nodded.

"Isn't that unusual?"

"One sold out, the other was cashiered." His lip curled again.

"Cashiered? You mean dismissed? Whatever for?"

"Dereliction of duty. He spent the Battle of Vimeiro in his billet, too drunk to stand up."

Letty nodded, and looked down at her hands. She plucked at the tip of one finger, pulling the glove. *Do I want to be involved in this?*

"The man who sold out is Reginald Grantham."

Letty's head jerked up. "Grantham?"

"A suitor of yours, I'm given to understand."

She nodded, mute.

"When you next see Grantham, could you ask him for me?" Reid's voice was neutral, almost diffident. "Please?"

His voice might be neutral, but nothing else was—the sharp-knuckled hands, the intensity of his gaze, the way he sat—stiff, leaning forward slightly. *This means a great deal to him.*

"Please?" Reid said again, and emotion leaked into his voice: a faint edge of desperation.

For some reason, that edge of desperation made her ribcage tighten. *He's begging.* Letty looked down at her own hands. "Were the scouts close friends of yours, Mr. Reid?"

Reid didn't speak for several seconds. "No. I barely knew them."

Letty glanced up. He was no longer leaning tensely forward. The intensity was gone from his face. He looked tired and ill and defeated. *He expects me to refuse.*

"What sort of men were they?"

"Good men. Brave men." His mouth tightened. "Peasants."

Did he think that that admission would make her less likely to help him? Yes, he did; he was pushing to his feet.

"Sit down, Mr. Reid."

Reid cast her a sharp glance, hesitated, and then sat again.

Letty looked back down at her hands, rather than his hopeful eyes. "How did you hear of my . . . knack?"

"A friend. He told me Grantham was at your feet, and that you'd be certain to kick him away because you always knew when your suitors were untruthful. He said you had an uncanny talent for distinguishing truth from lies."

"Which friend?"

"Colonel Winton."

Letty saw the colonel in her mind's eye—stocky, graying, hawk-eyed—and nodded. "Tell me about yourself."

There was a pause. She glanced up to see Reid's brow wrinkle. "Me?"

"Who are you, Mr. Reid?"

Another pause, and then Reid said, "My father was Sir Hector Reid of Yorkshire. I'm the youngest of five sons. I joined the Thirty-third Foot as an ensign. Flanders first, then India." His delivery was flat and unemotional. "After the Battle of Mallavelly, Wellesley took me for one of his aides. I was on his staff for five years, then Gore's. Wellesley requested me back for Copenhagen. After Copenhagen, we were to sail to South America, but we were sent to Portugal instead."

"What's your rank?"

Another pause. "I was a major."

"You've been invalided out?"

"I resigned my commission."

"Because of what happened in Portugal?"

"Yes."

Letty studied his face. A career soldier didn't resign his commission because of the deaths of three peasants he barely knew. "Something else happened, didn't it?"

Reid's face tightened. "Yes."

"What?"

Reid's face became even tighter. He didn't speak.

"Major Reid, if you're not truthful with me—"

"It's not fit for your ears," he said flatly.

Letty closed her mouth, hearing the bell-like chime of truth in his words. Something terrible had happened in Portugal. Something terrible enough to make this man resign his commission.

She studied Major Reid's face—the skin stretched taut over his bones, the tension, the exhaustion. She'd been right to think there was something seriously wrong with him. He was brittle, ready to break.

Up in the ballroom, the musicians stopped playing. The *contredanse* was over. It was time for her to leave the conservatory and find her next partner.

Letty stayed seated. "Who is the second man?"

"George Dunlop."

"I don't know him."

"He's in Marshalsea."

Letty jerked slightly. "Prison?"

"He's a debtor."

"Major Reid, I can't . . ." Letty shook her head silently. *I can't enter a prison!*

Reid leaned forward on his chair. The tension and the fierce hope were gone. He looked drained. More exhausted than anyone she'd ever seen. "Miss Trentham, I'll be dead before the end of the year and I need to make this right before I die. Please, will you help me?"

Letty stared at him, hearing the truth in his words. Muscles constricted in her throat, but she wasn't entirely certain why. Because Reid was dying? Because he was begging? Both? "Of course I'll help," she heard herself say.

Reid closed his eyes briefly. "Thank you." He exhaled a low breath and straightened in the chair, but his exhaustion didn't ease. Everything about him was weary—his long limbs, his gaunt face, his silver eyes. Even his hands were weary, no longer clenched.

"But you must promise not to kill the traitor."

Reid's eyebrows came sharply together. The weariness evaporated. He was suddenly taut, tense, dangerous.

"I will *not* be responsible for deciding whether a man lives or dies," Letty said firmly. "A military court is the place for that."

Reid stared at her for a long moment, his eyes boring into

her—and then he gave a stiff nod. "Very well."

"You must *promise* me you won't kill him. On your word of honor."

"You have my word of honor I won't kill him." The words came from his mouth reluctantly, but they were the truth.

Letty almost wished he had refused. Did she *really* want to be involved in this? "I ride in Hyde Park most afternoons. Meet me there tomorrow. I'll ask Grantham to join me."

"Will he come?"

"I'm the heiress he's angling to marry," she said tartly. "Of course he'll come."

Reid's eyebrows lifted slightly at her tone, but he made no comment.

"You may ask Grantham your questions; I'll tell you whether he's lying or not."

"You *will* be able to tell?"

Letty nodded.

"How?"

"I hear it."

"This knack of yours, is it . . ." His brow creased as he searched for a word. "Infallible?"

"I hear every single lie, Major Reid."

He frowned. "How?"

A gift from my Faerie godmother. Letty shrugged lightly. "A quirk of my birth. You may test me tomorrow, if you disbelieve me." She stood. "Now, you must excuse me; I'm engaged for this dance."

Reid stood, too.

"Three o'clock at the Grosvenor Gate."

"Thank you."

Letty could think of no suitable reply. *You're welcome,* and *It's my pleasure,* were both lies. She settled for a nod.

She climbed the shallow steps and emerged into the ballroom

with a sense of having woken from a disturbing dream. *This* was normalcy—the rustle of expensive fabric and glitter of jewels, the scents of dozens of different perfumes, the babble of voices, the gaiety. The fortune hunters.

Letty glanced back, almost expecting Major Reid to have disappeared. But no, he stood in the conservatory, tall and gaunt, watching her. With a black cloak and scythe, he'd be the Grim Reaper.

And I have agreed to help him. Not smart, Letitia. Not smart at all.

Letty shivered, and set out across the dance floor in search of Lord Stapleton.

Like to read the rest?
Trusting Miss Trentham is available now.

ACKNOWLEDGMENTS

A NUMBER OF people helped to make this book what it is. I would like to thank my editors, Laura Cifelli Stibich and Bev Katz Rosenbaum, my copyeditor, Maria Fairchild, and my proofreader, Martin O'Hearn.

The cover and the series logo are both the work of the talented Kim Killion, of The Killion Group. Thank you, Kim!

And last—but definitely not least—my thanks go to my parents, without whose support this book would not have been published.

Emily Larkin grew up in a house full of books—her mother was a librarian and her father a novelist—so perhaps it's not surprising that she became a writer.

Emily has studied a number of subjects, including geology and geophysics, canine behavior, and ancient Greek. Her varied career includes stints as a field assistant in Antarctica and a waitress on the Isle of Skye, as well as five vintages in New Zealand's wine industry.

She loves to travel and has lived in Sweden, backpacked in Europe and North America, and traveled overland in the Middle East, China, and North Africa. She enjoys climbing hills, yoga workouts, watching reruns of *Buffy the Vampire Slayer* and *Firefly,* and reading.

Emily writes historical romances as Emily Larkin and fantasy novels as Emily Gee. Her websites are www.emilylarkin.com and www.emilygee.com.

Never miss a new Emily Larkin book! Join her Readers' Group at www.emilylarkin.com/newsletter and receive free digital copies of *The Fey Quartet* and *Unmasking Miss Appleby*.

Printed in Great Britain
by Amazon

41760389R00095